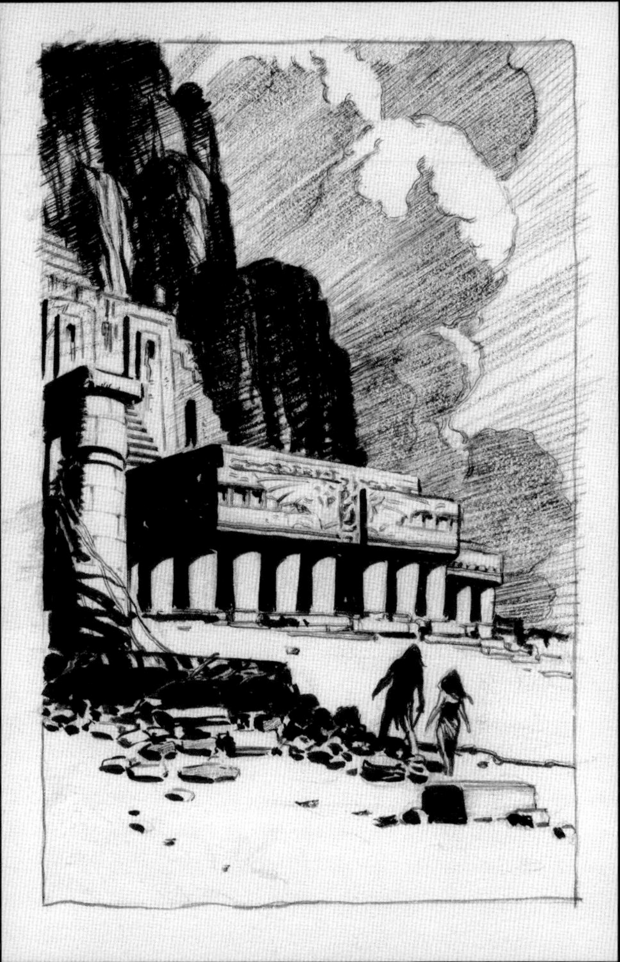

MW01705854

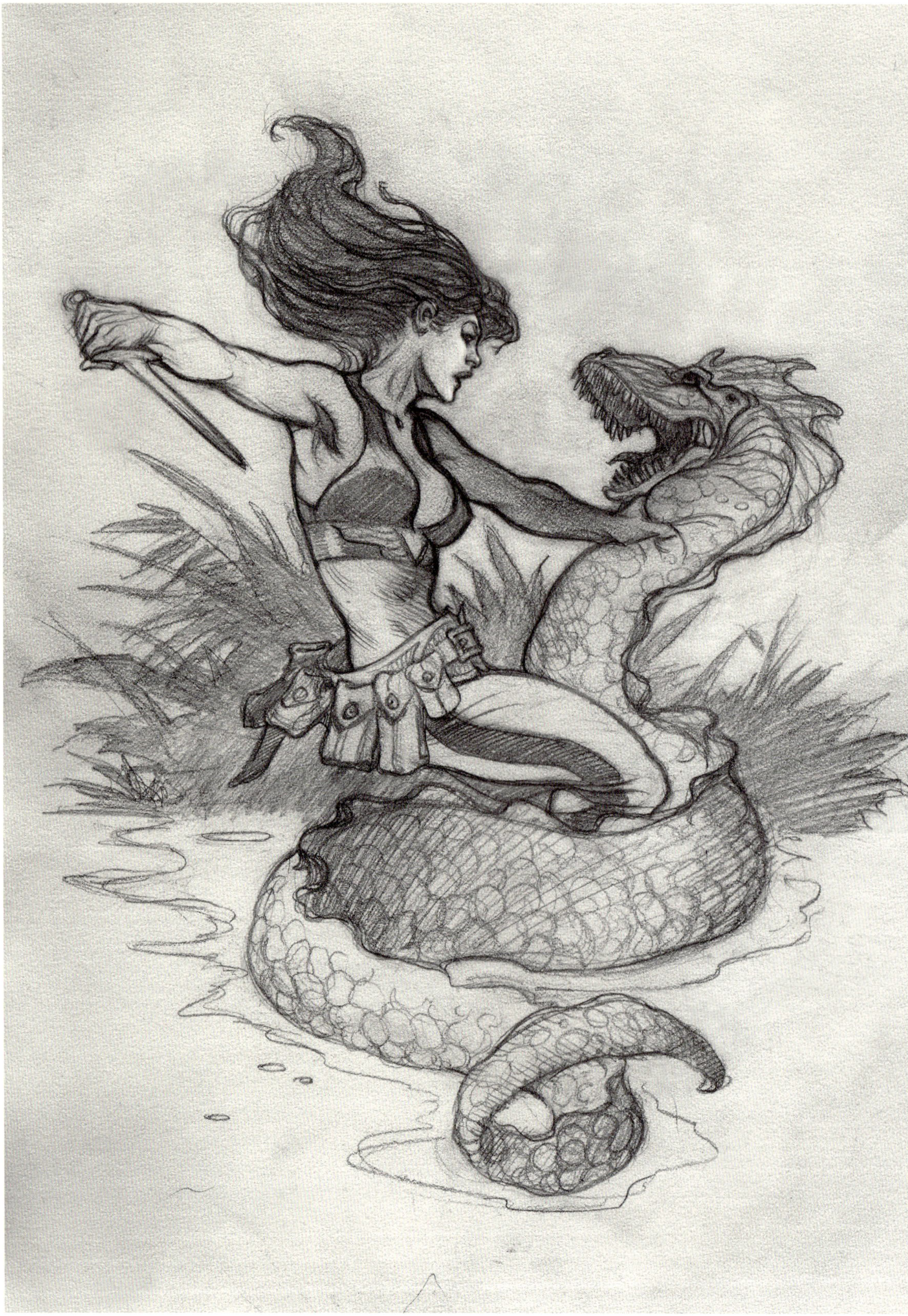

MARK SCHULTZ

Various Drawings

A COLLECTION OF STUDIES AND FINISHED WORKS

Flesk Publications™

A BREAKER HOUSE™ PRODUCTION

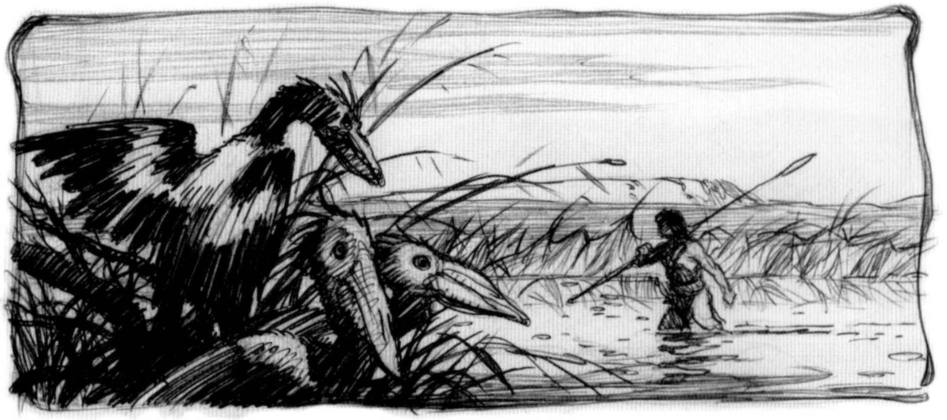

Designed by Randall Dahlk

Thanks to John Fleskes for the initial scans and tutorials, and to Mike and Priscilla Blanchard for supplying additional scans from their collection.- M.S.
Thanks to Jim Keegan for his constant assistance.- J.F.

First Printing
July 2005

Softbound Edition ISBN: 0-9723758-6-4
Hardbound Limited Signed and Numbered Edition ISBN: 0-9723758-7-2

Printed in Hong Kong

Also available from Flesk Publications:
Franklin Booth: Painter with a Pen
Joseph Clement Coll: The Art of Adventure
Joseph Clement Coll: A Legacy in Line

Flesk Publications™
P.O. Box 3174 Santa Cruz, CA 95063
www.fleskpublications.com info@fleskpublications.com

VARIOUS DRAWINGS INTRODUCTION

I'm not exactly sure why, but I've always felt, at best, ambivalent about putting my preliminaries, roughs and studies on public display.

The great 19th century American painter Thomas Eakins felt that his finished canvases should speak for themselves and directed that his preliminary drawings be destroyed upon his death.

His directions weren't followed, and maybe we're all the better for the insights rescued for our edification, but I sympathize with Eakins' wishes. Part of me wants the back stage machinations to remain hidden, to keep the end result all that more magical. Who are we to second-guess Thomas Eakins?

More likely, my reticence concerning my own work has to do with personal insecurities. None of my drawings is ever quite "right" in my mind, whether finish or study. All contain a host of mistakes and problematic solutions that could be corrected if only there were *a little more time.* I'm never quite ready to let them go.

Not the healthiest mental state, I admit, but there you have it. Releasing finishes is painful enough. A book primarily comprised of preliminaries, which were created only in service to a work in progress, could be murder.

Fortunately—for me, that is—my anxieties are balanced by an appreciation for the law of supply and demand and an essentially capitalistic pragmatism. I have been happily convinced that there are patrons out there willing to overlook my drafting flaws, and among them there exists enough prepared to shell out for a volume of my scribblings. Opportunism and avarice have once again triumphed over rectitude and self-deprecation, and you hold the result in your hands.

But enough about *me*—let me draw your attention to the drawings.

There are actually plenty of finishes distributed between the preliminary works herein, and most of those have never before been published, either. I've left all the pieces I decided to include as is—I've resisted the temptation to pick up pencil and brush and pretty them up for publication.

Well, okay—I've resisted in most cases. I grudgingly admit that I digitally "enhanced" a few, but the majority has been left to stand as I originally drew them, warts and all, as merely stages in a process. I swear.

Captions have been added only where I felt they were needed.

For anyone interested in a more sequential glimpse at how the process of creating a work proceeds, there are two centerpieces—the *Centrosaurus from Southern Alberta* and the *Blanchard Family Picnic*—that are accompanied by thumbnails and studies that took them from concept to completion.

If you are interested in such things.

Regardless, I hope you enjoy this, my first collection of drawings.

Mark Schultz
April, 2005

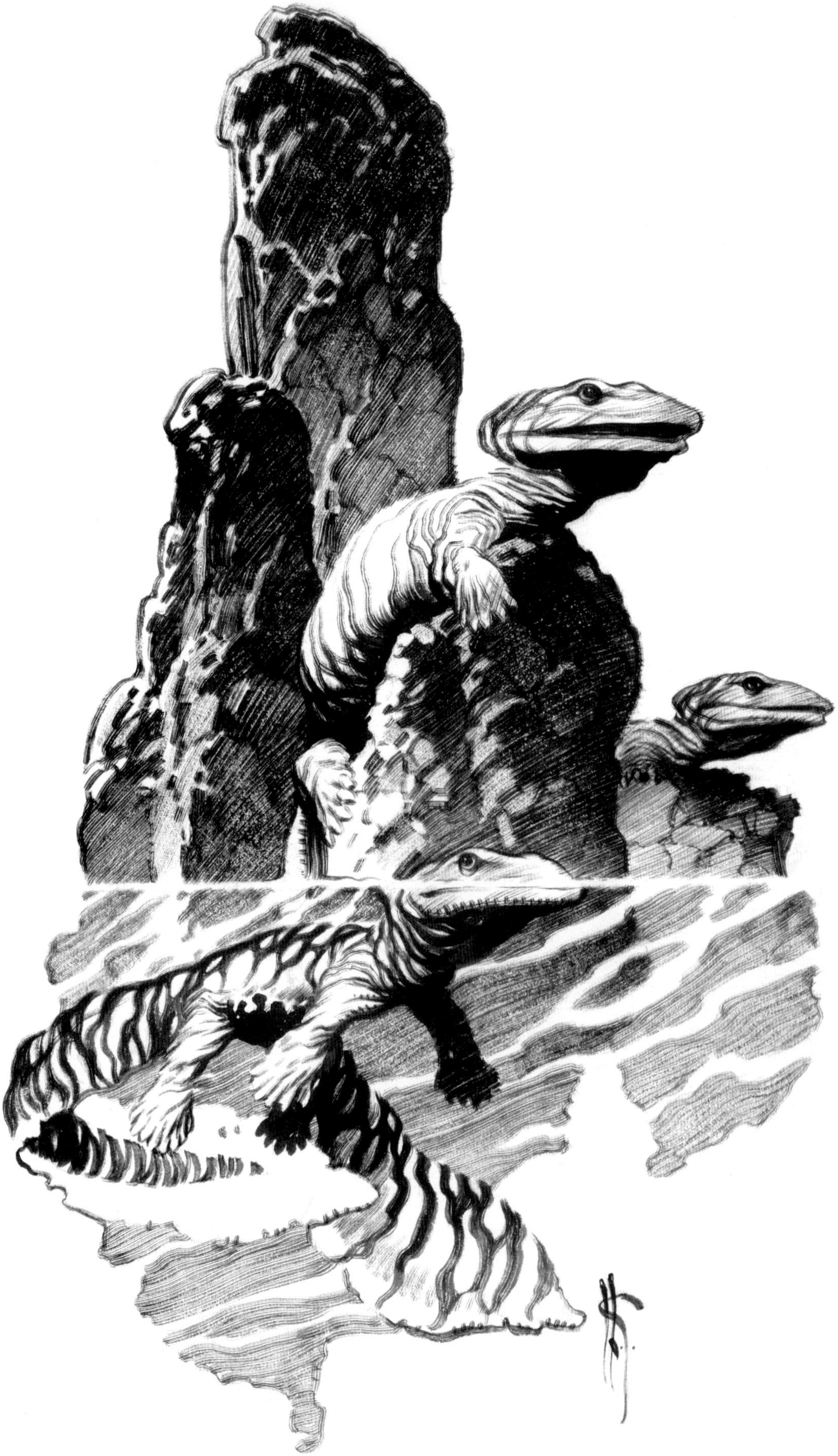

Acanthostega, a Devonian period amphibian. Possibly the first vertebrate to crawl out of the water and onto dry land

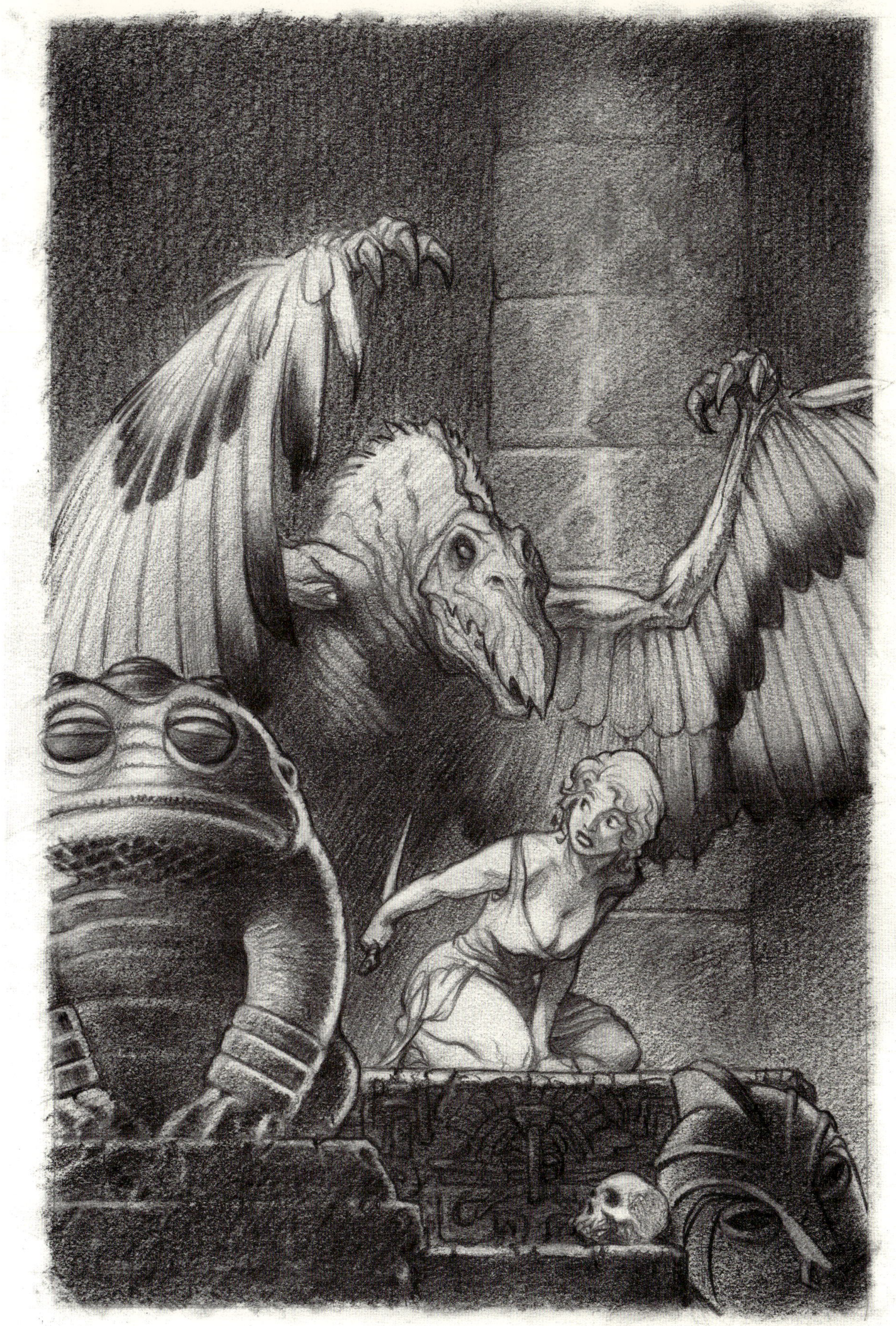

Preliminary for cover illustration for the forth-coming comic adventure series *Strange Passages*

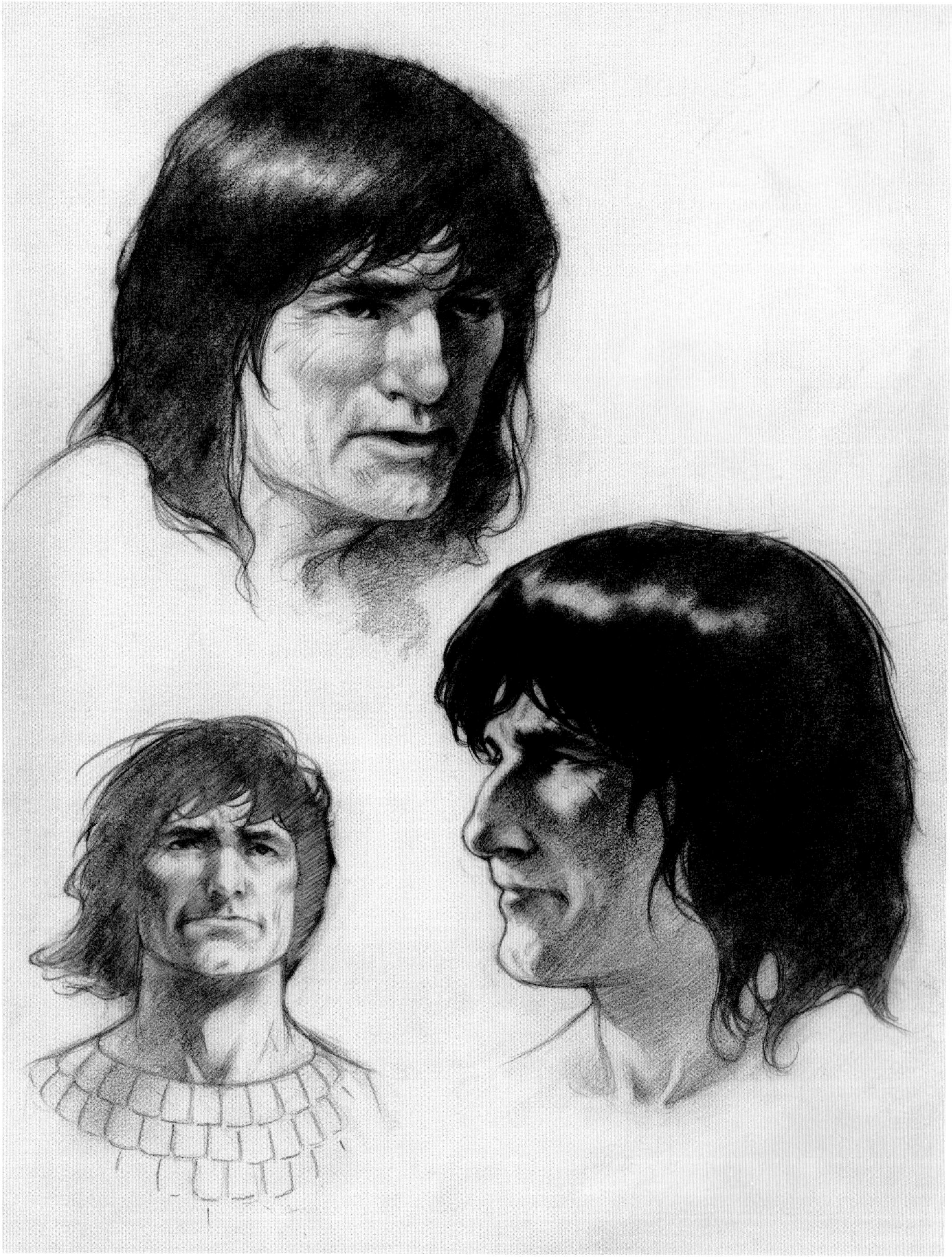

Concept models of Conan, preparation for *Robert E. Howard's Complete Conan of Cimmeria, Volume 1*

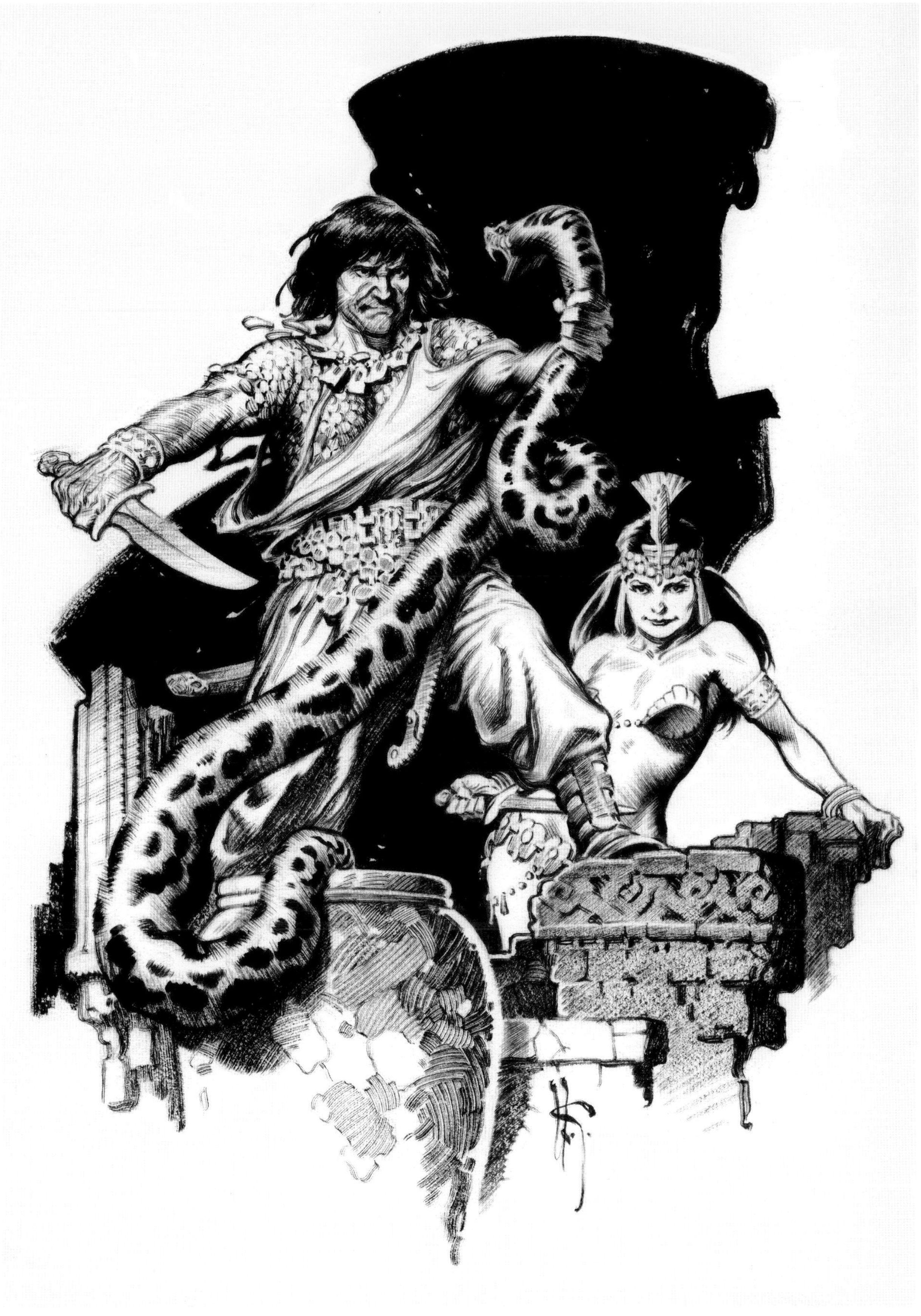

Bud Plant Comic Art bookplate illustration:
The Coming of Conan the Cimmerian

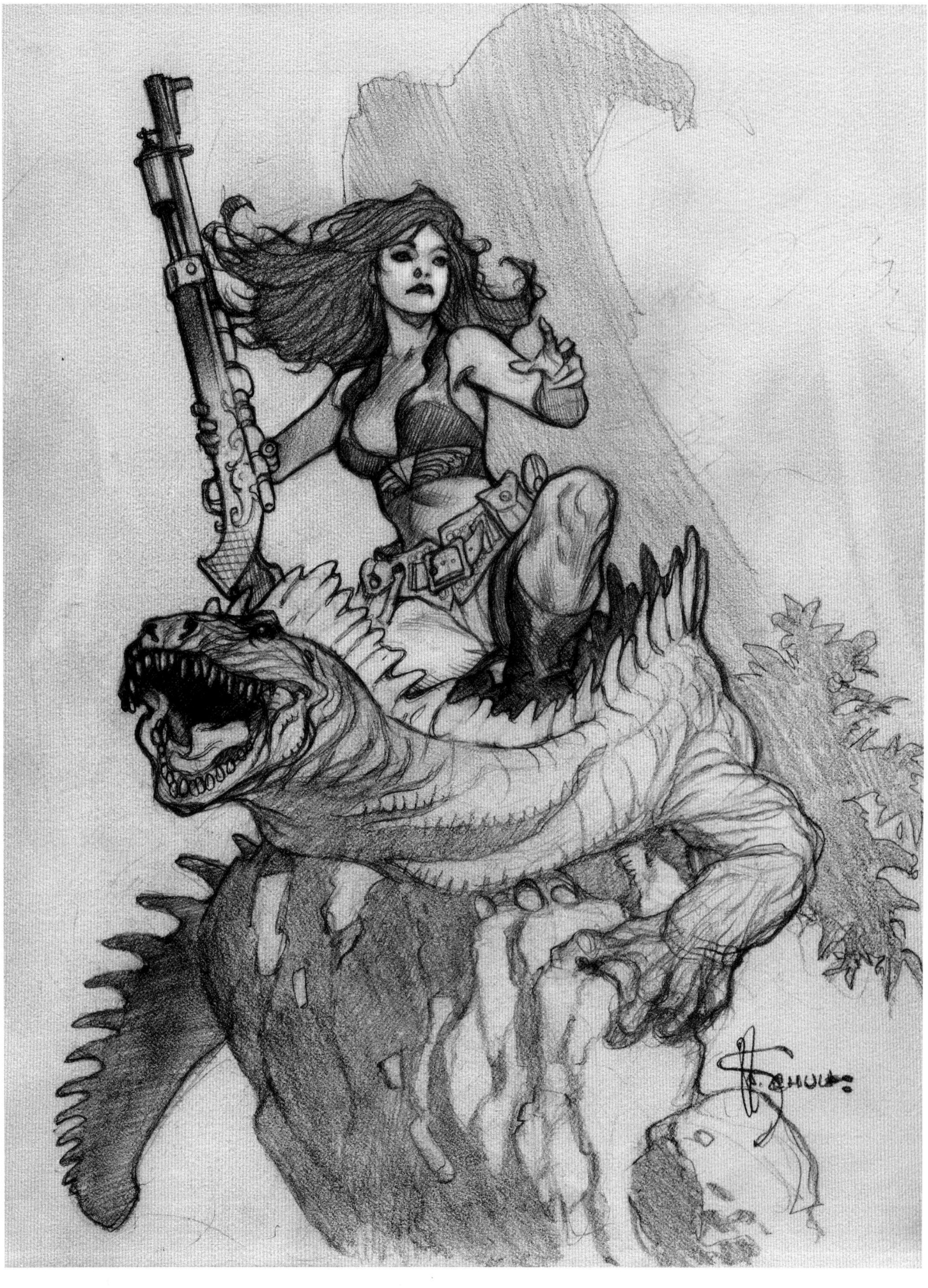

Hannah Dundee preliminary study...

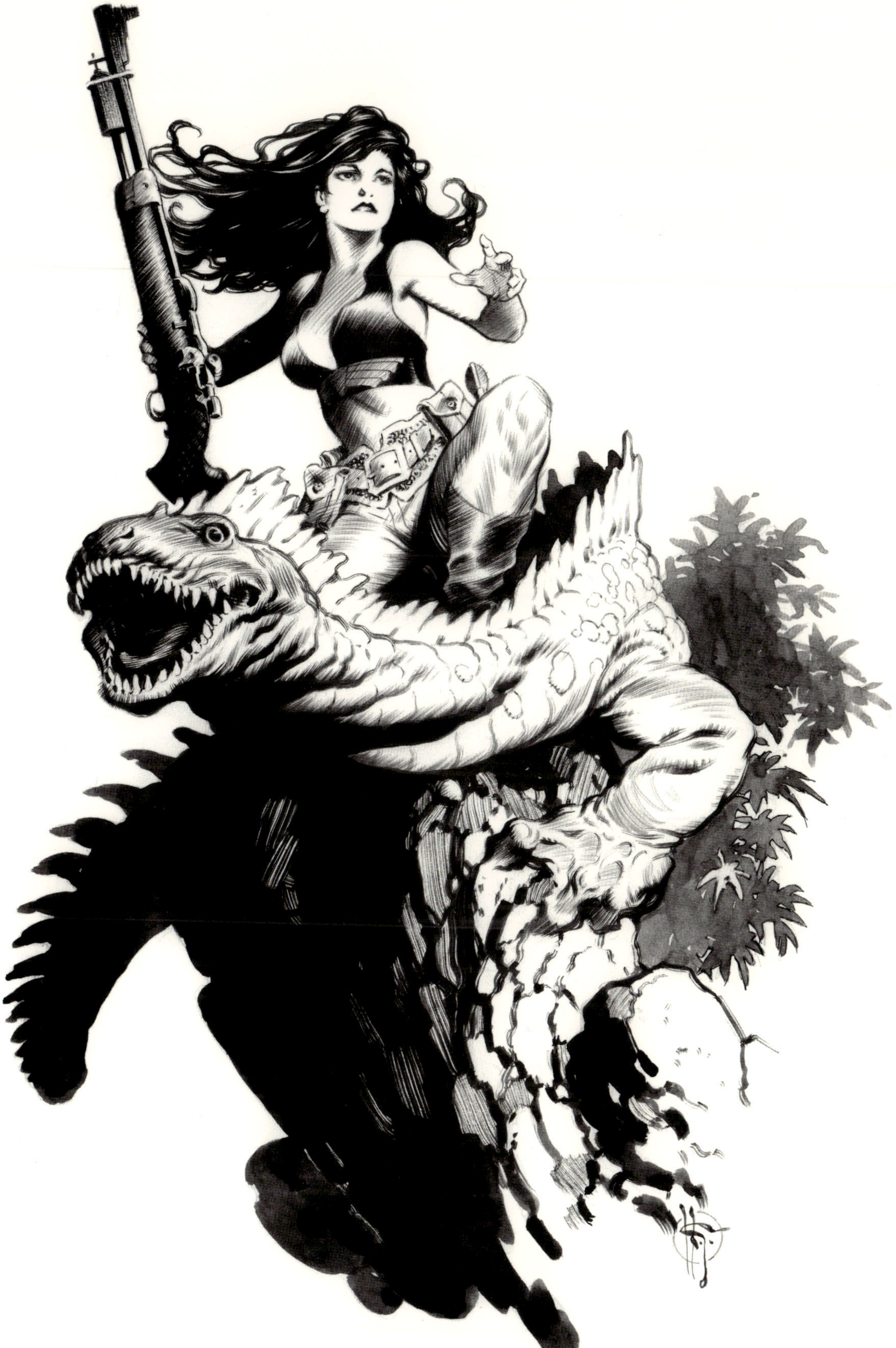

...And finish

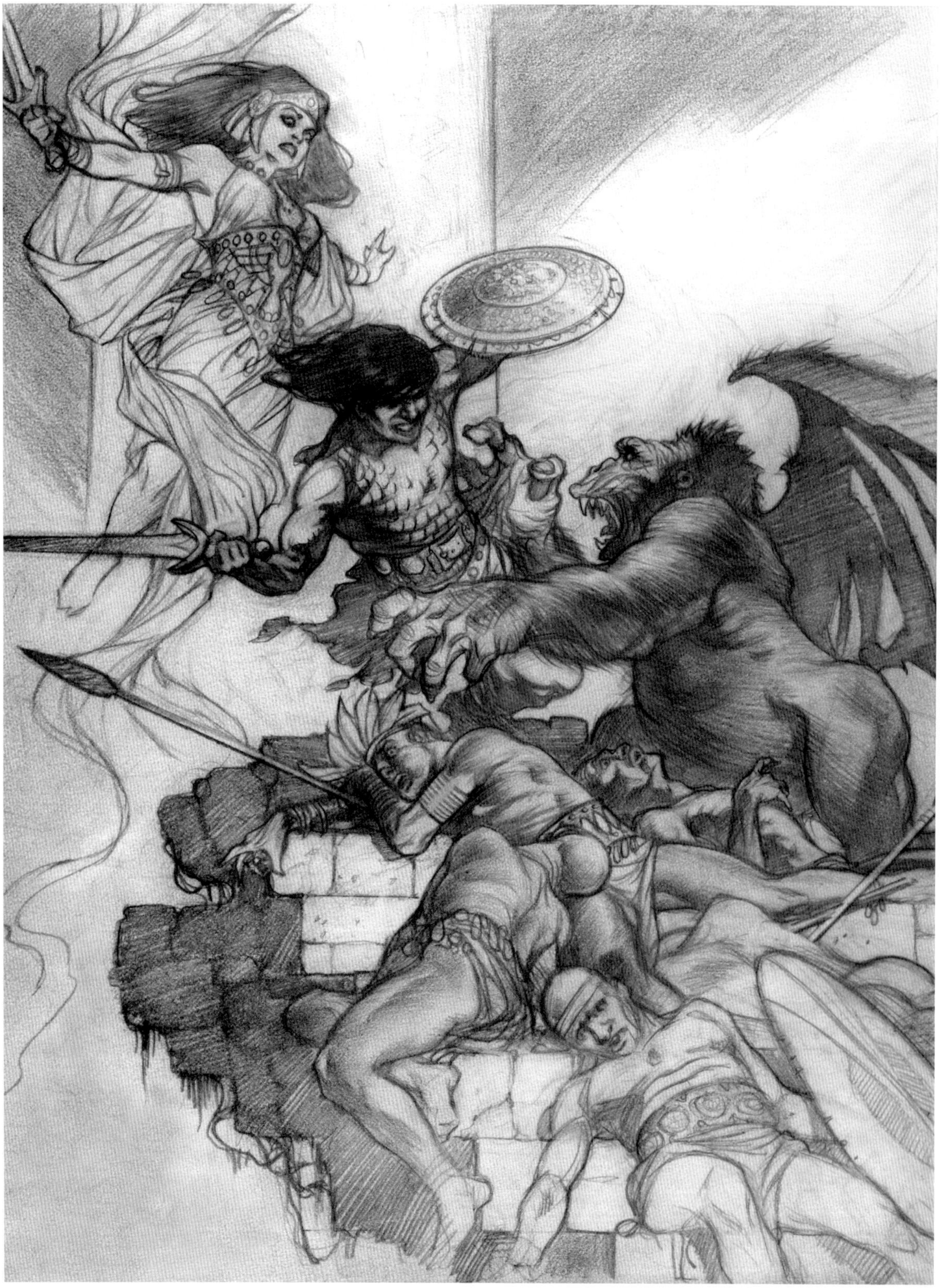

Study: Robert E. Howard's *Queen of the Black Coast*

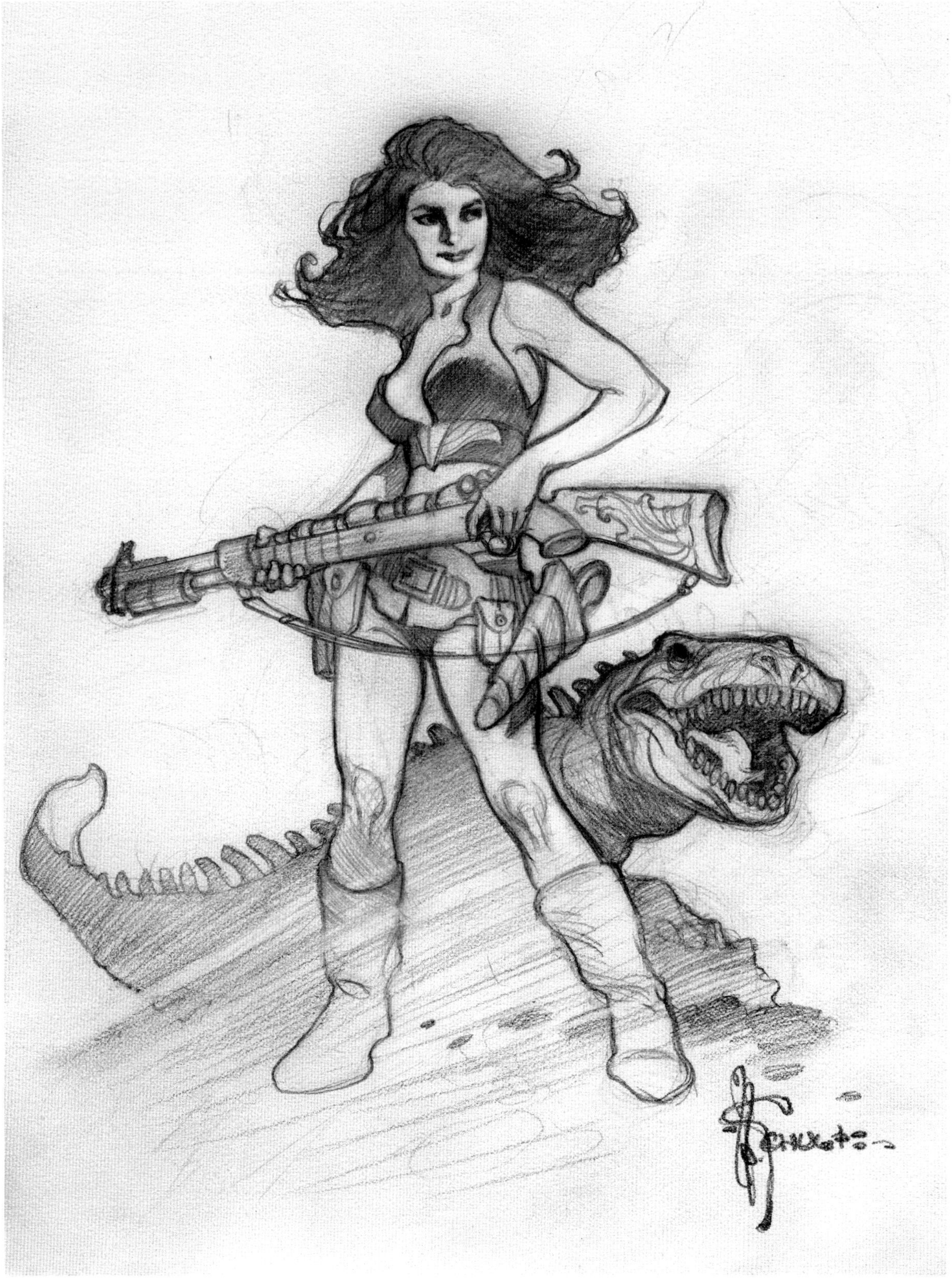

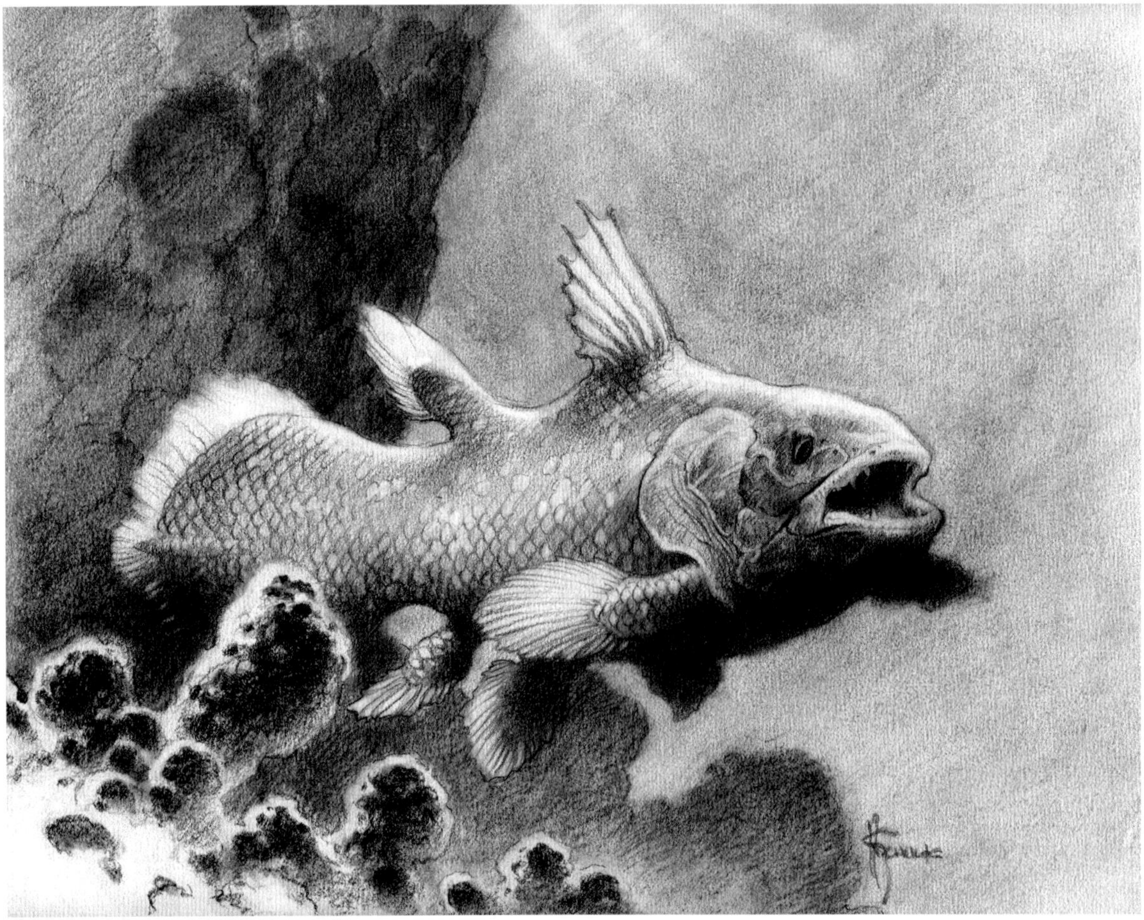

Latimeria chalumnae

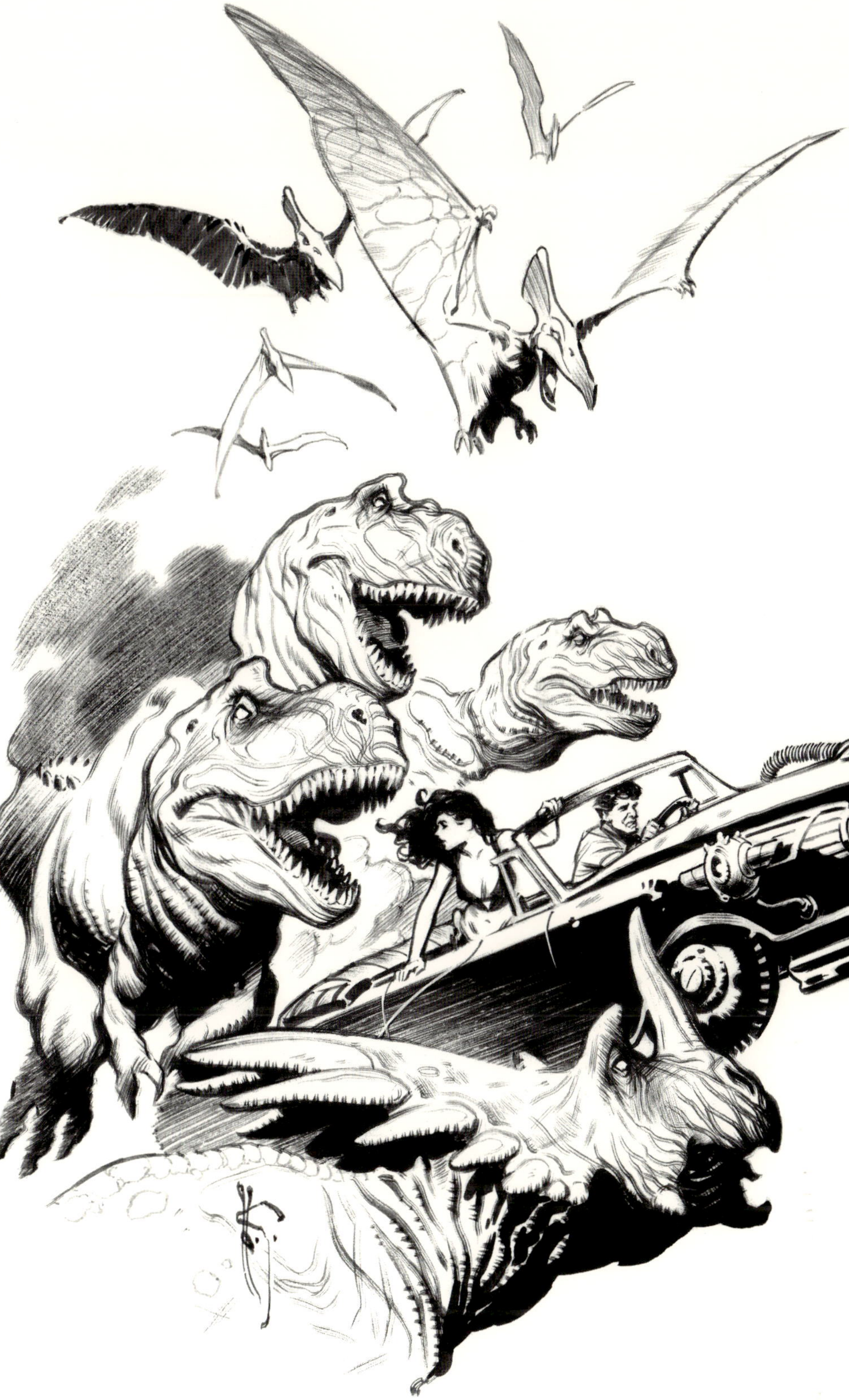

Bud Plant Comic Art envelope illustration: *Xenozoic Tales*

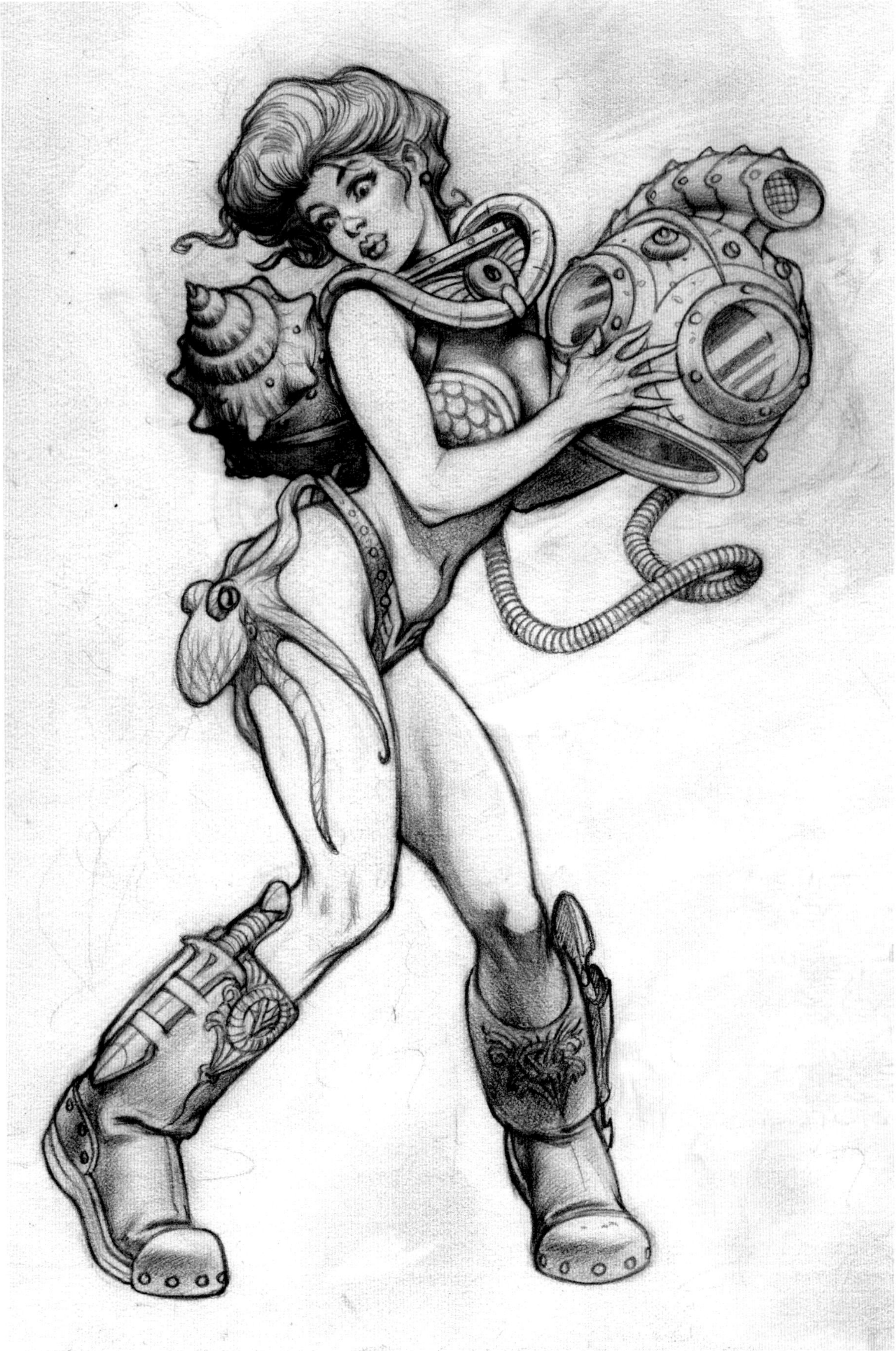

Concept art: Clayburn Moore's "Nemo Girl" limited edition sculpture

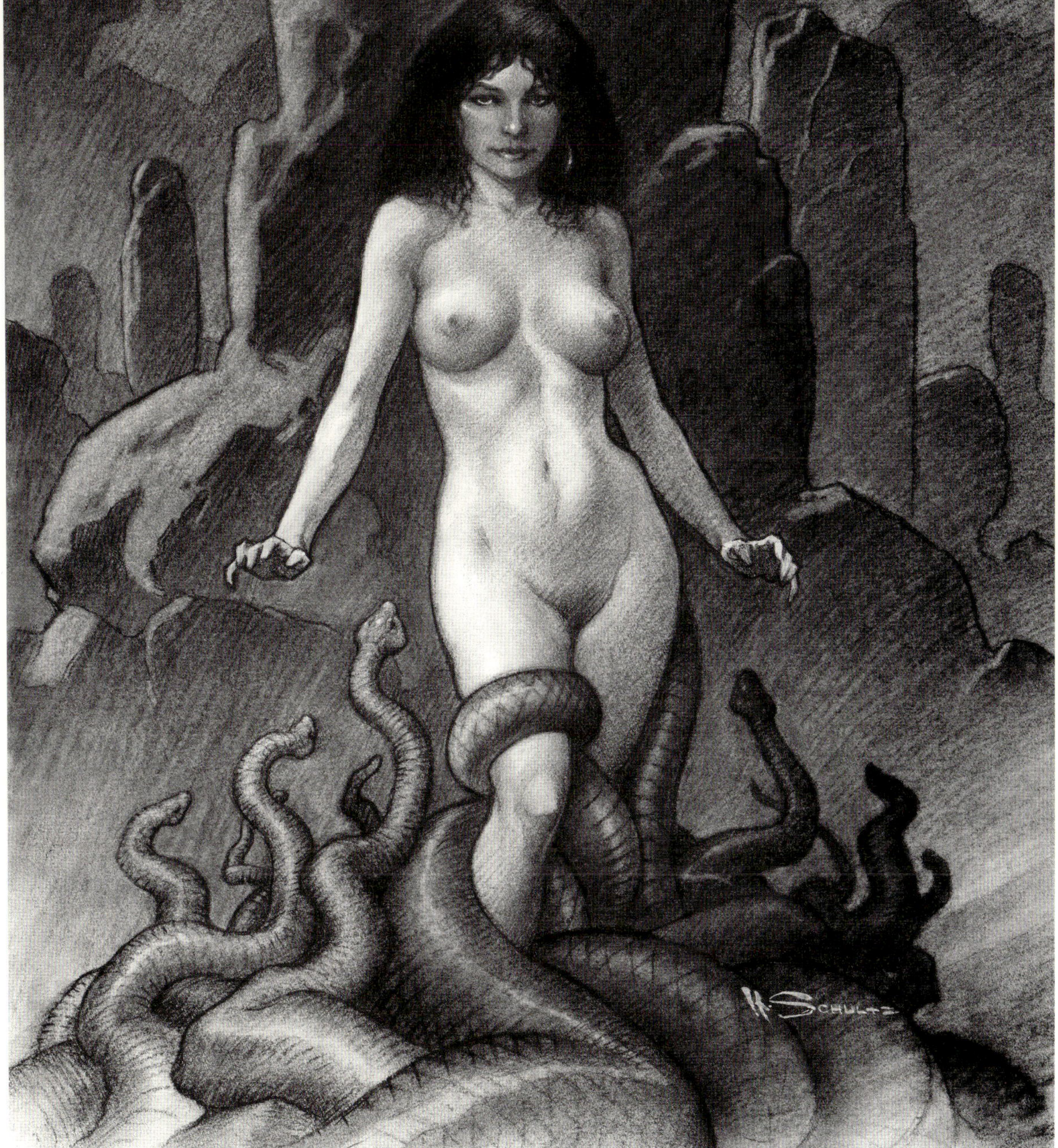

Hecate

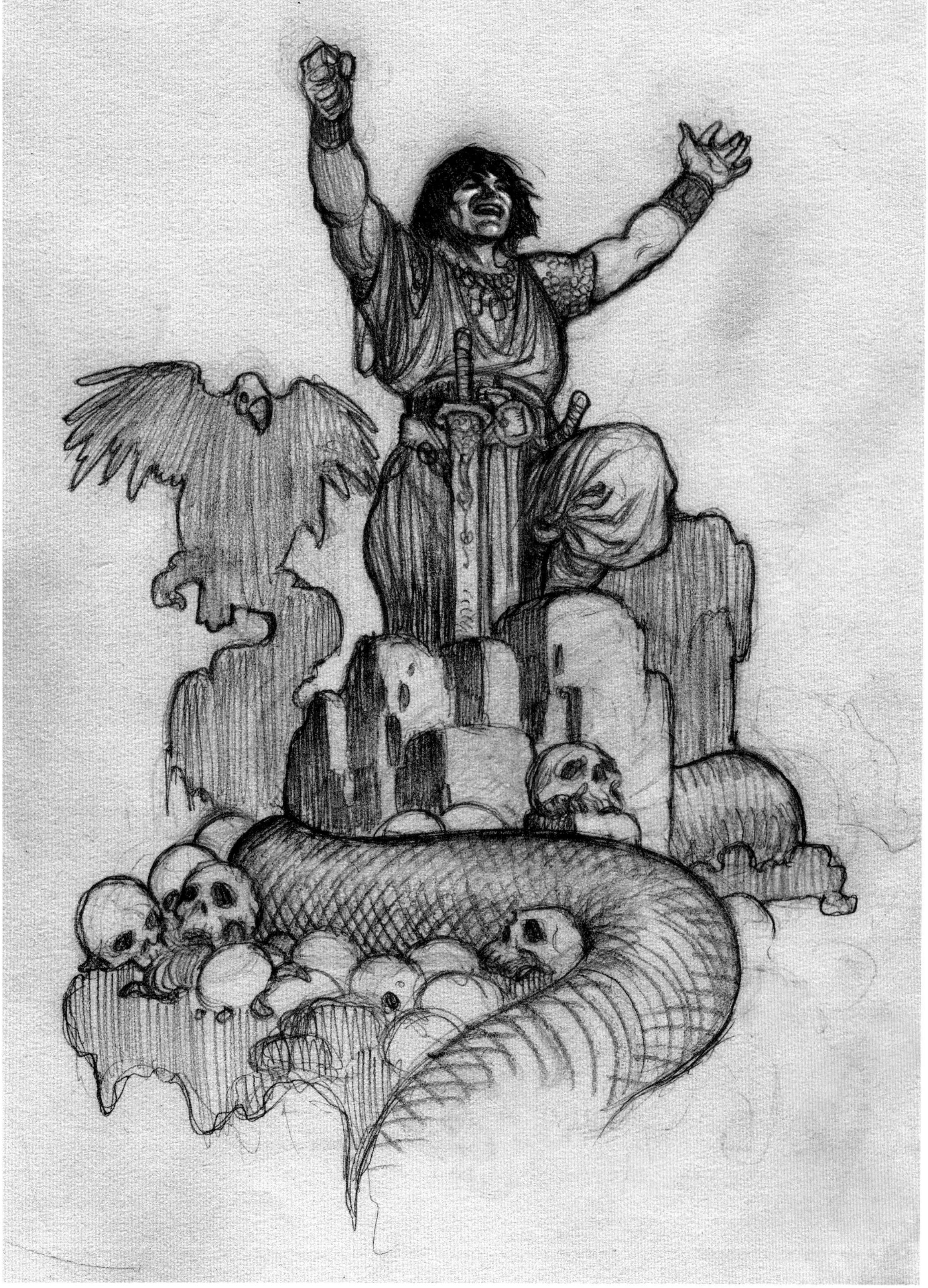

Title page illustration preliminary:
Robert E. Howard's Complete Conan of Cimmeria, Volume 1

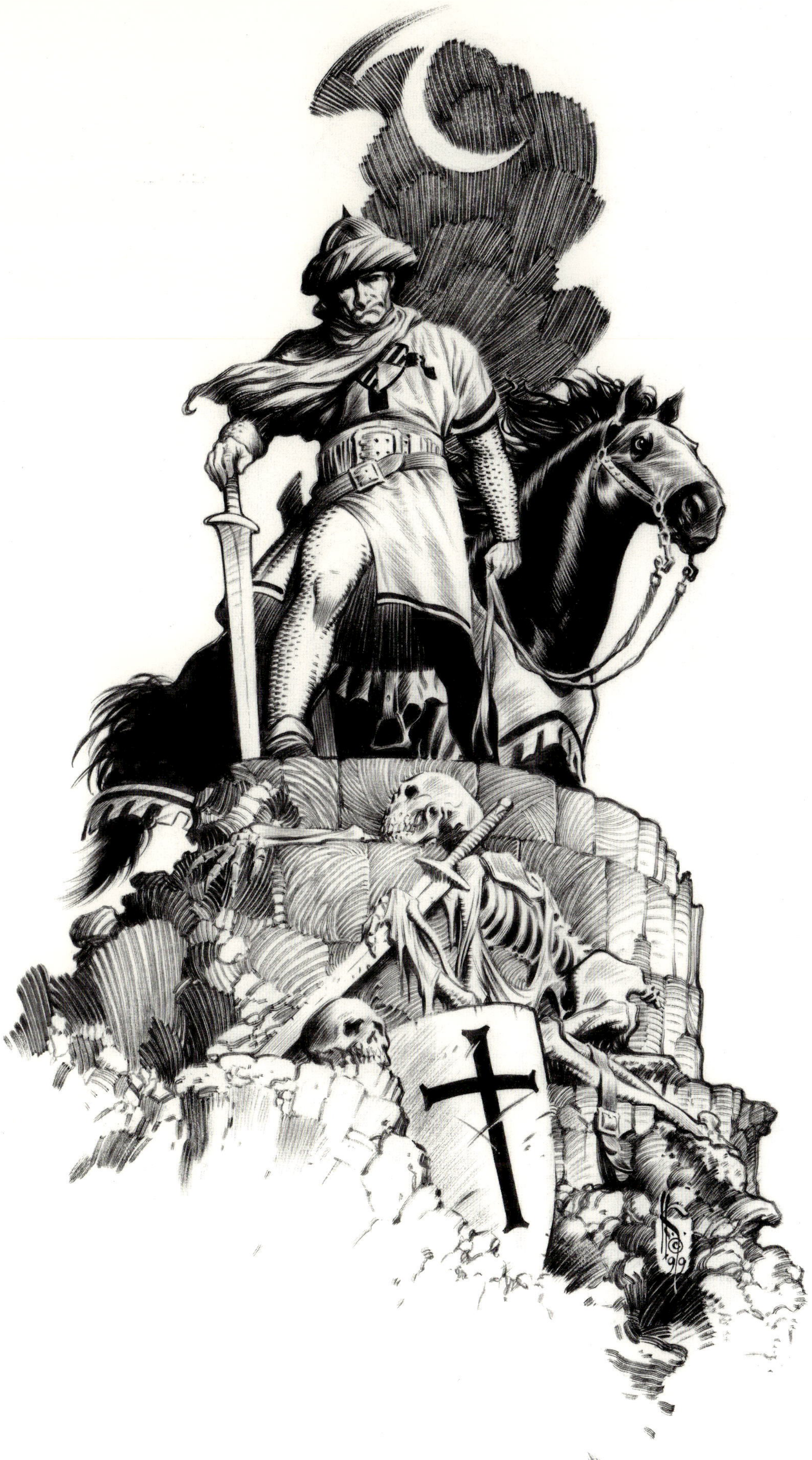

Crusader

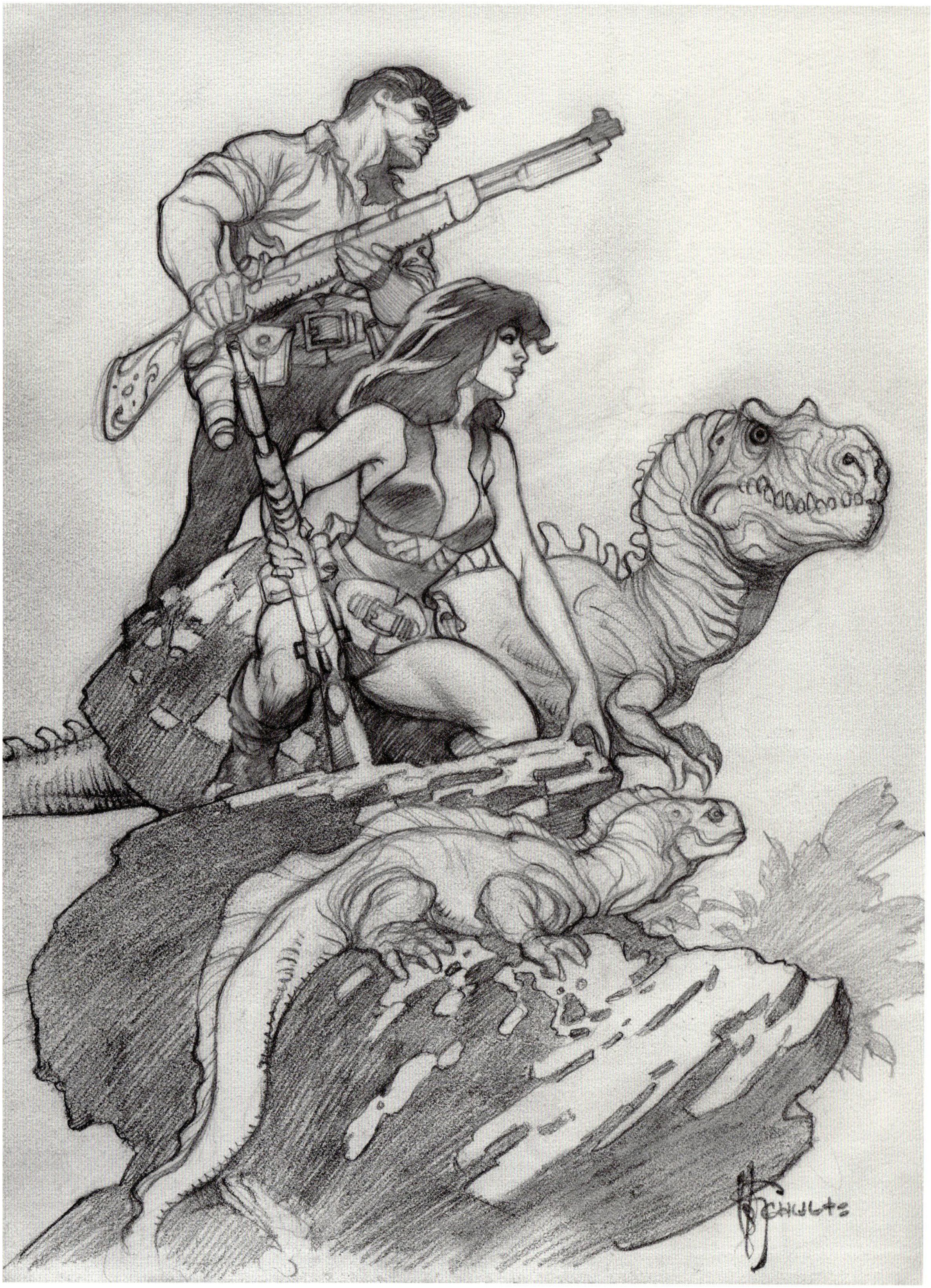

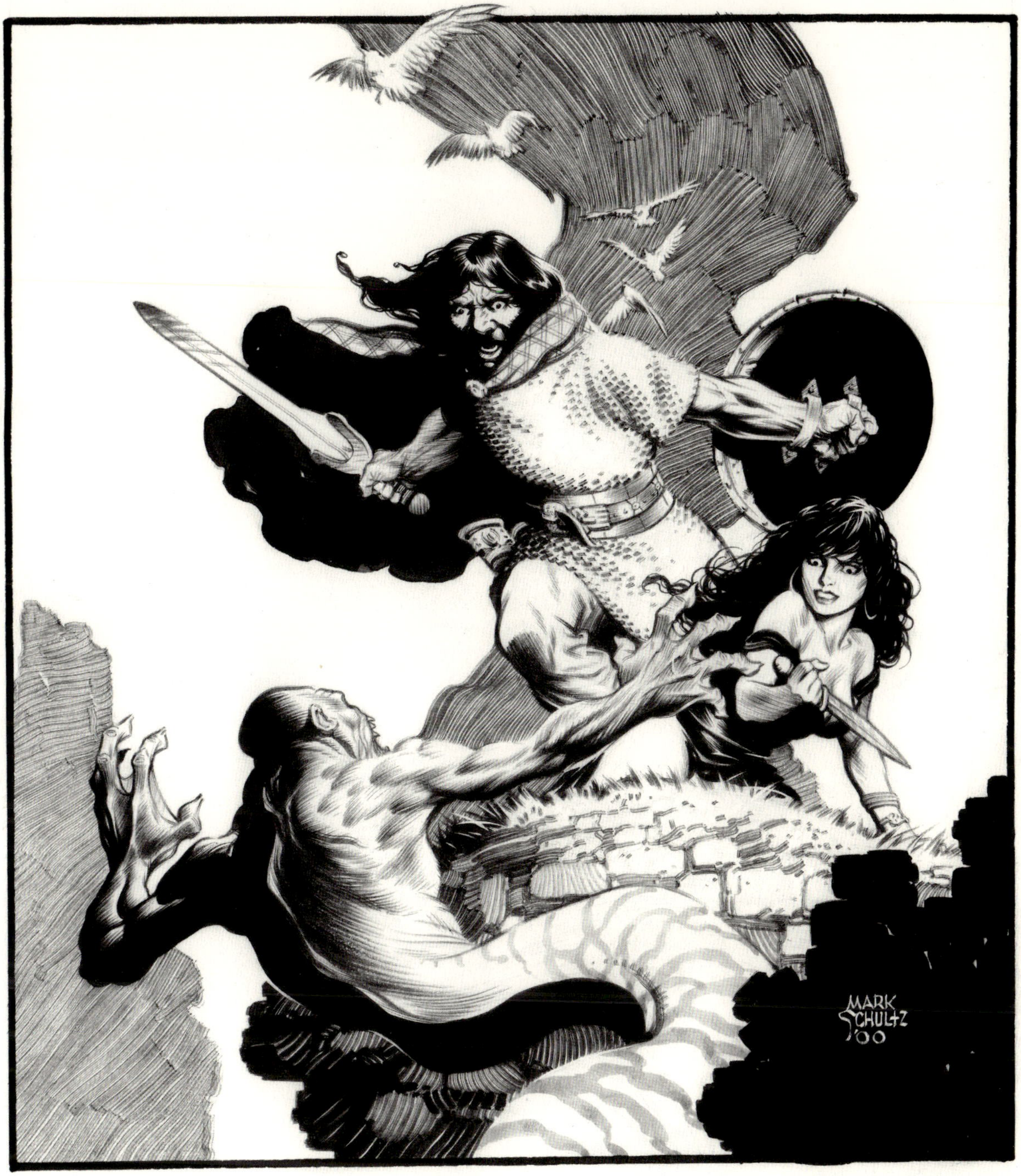

Cover illustration: Robert E. Howard's *Worms of the Earth*

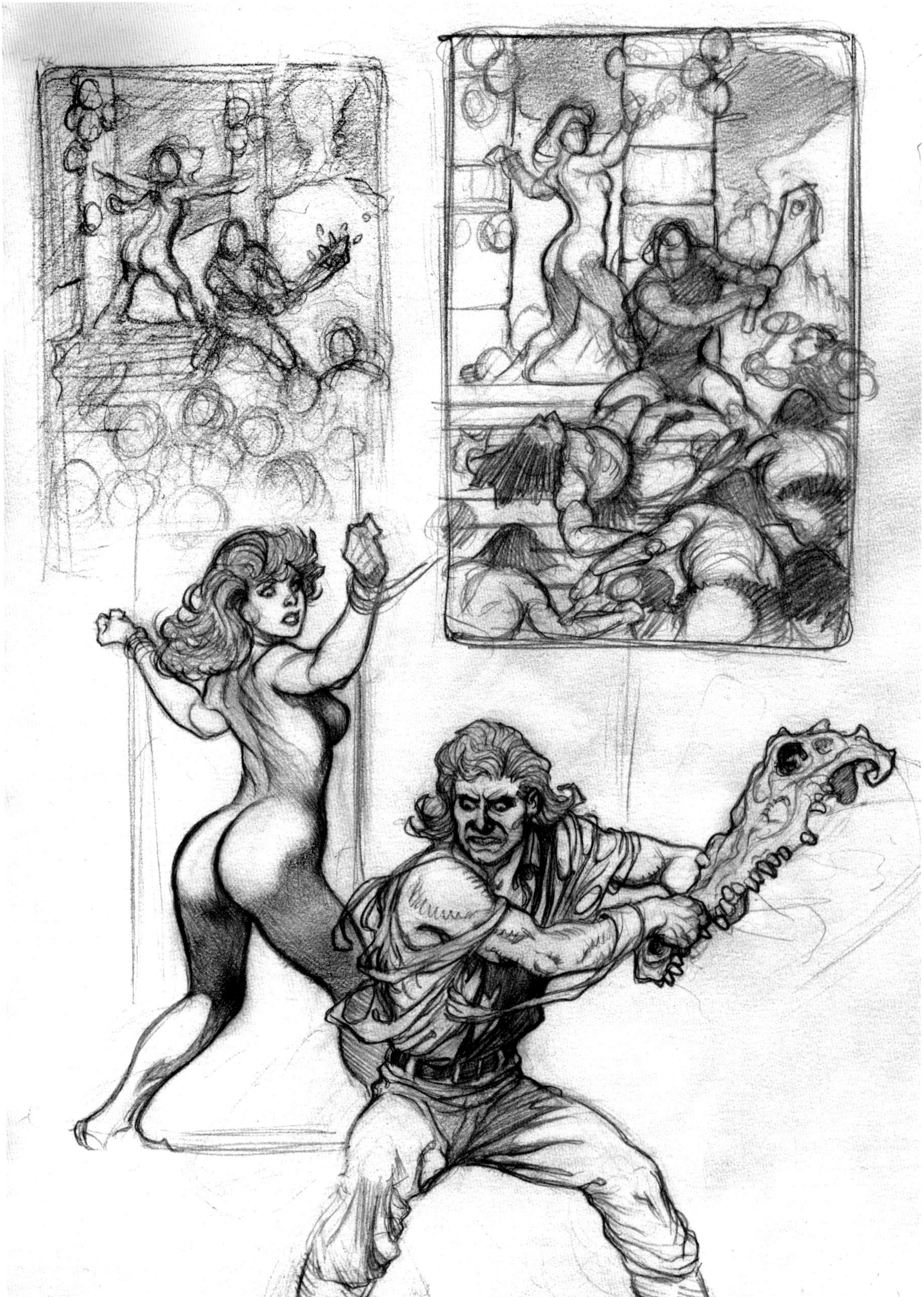

Sketchbook thumbnails and preliminary studies:
Blanchard Family Picnic

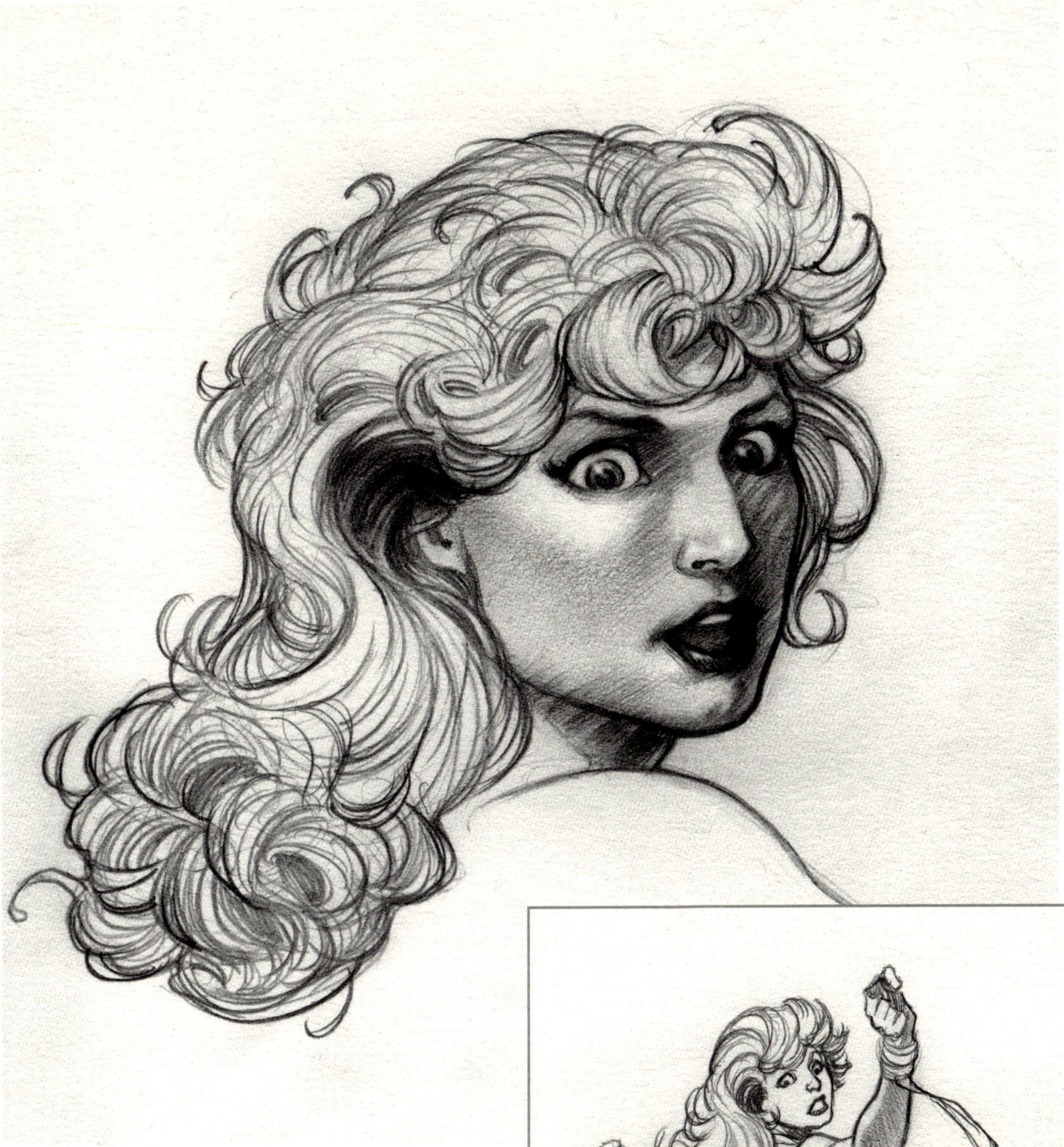

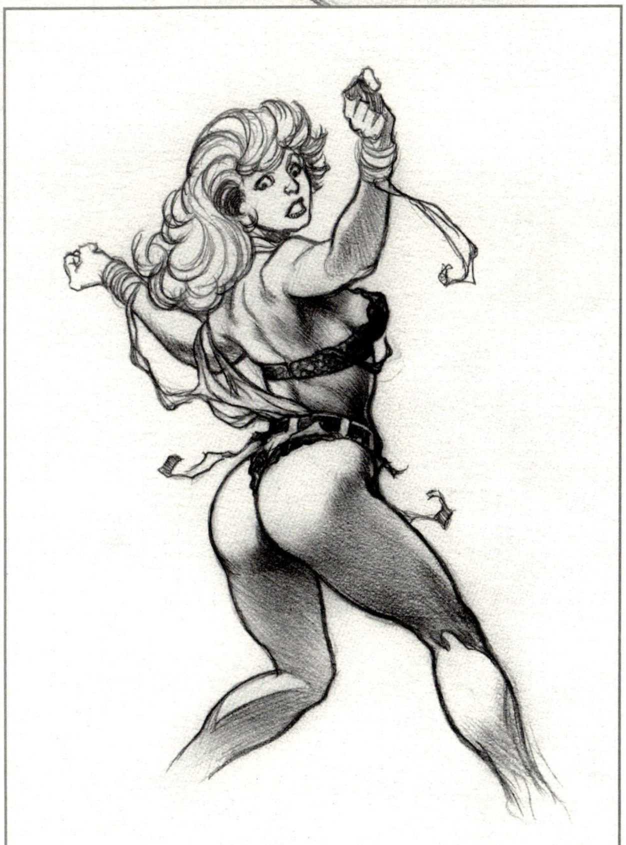

Model studies: *Blanchard Family Picnic*

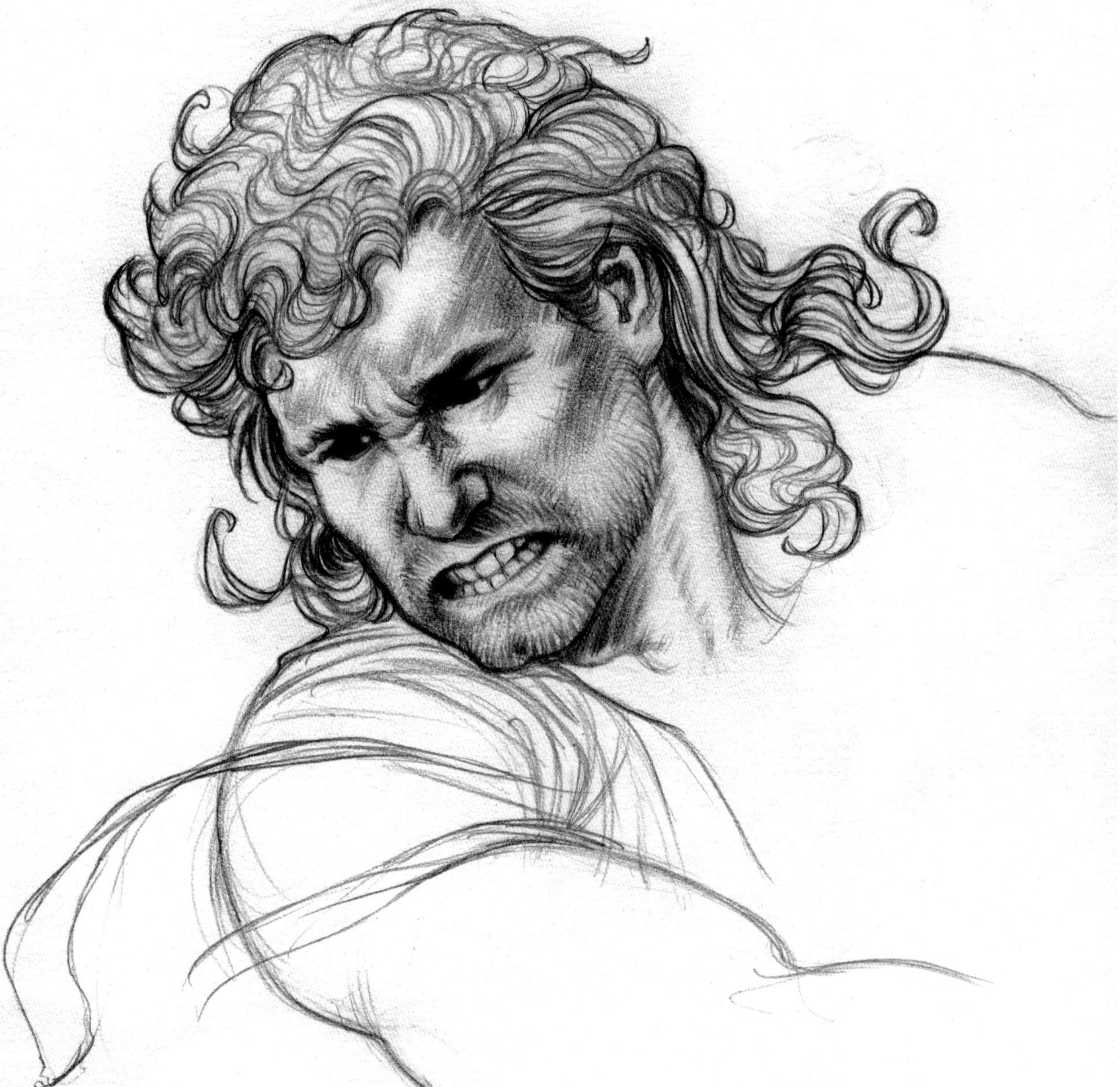

Model study: *Blanchard Family Picnic*

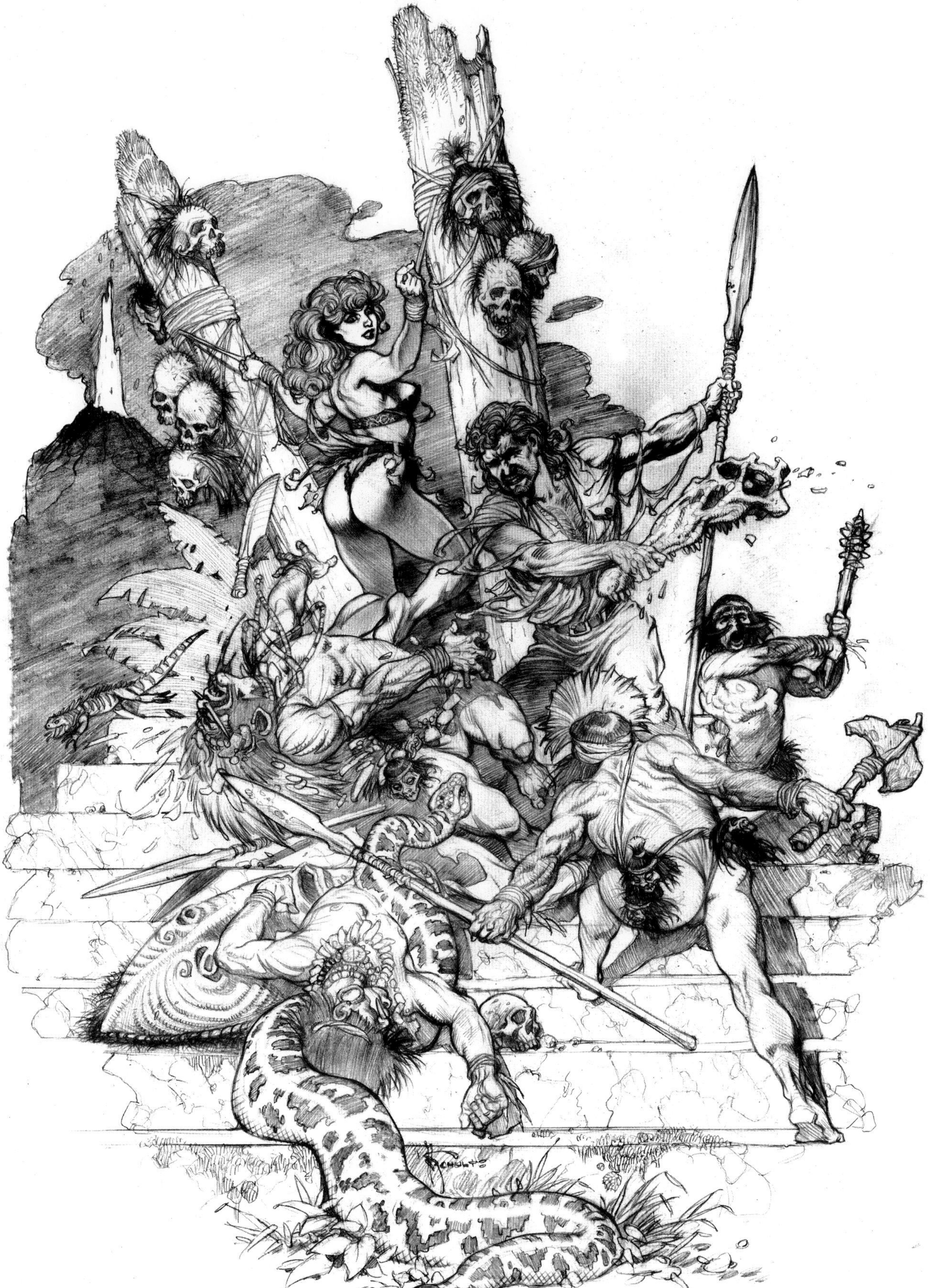

Final underdrawing: *Blanchard Family Picnic*

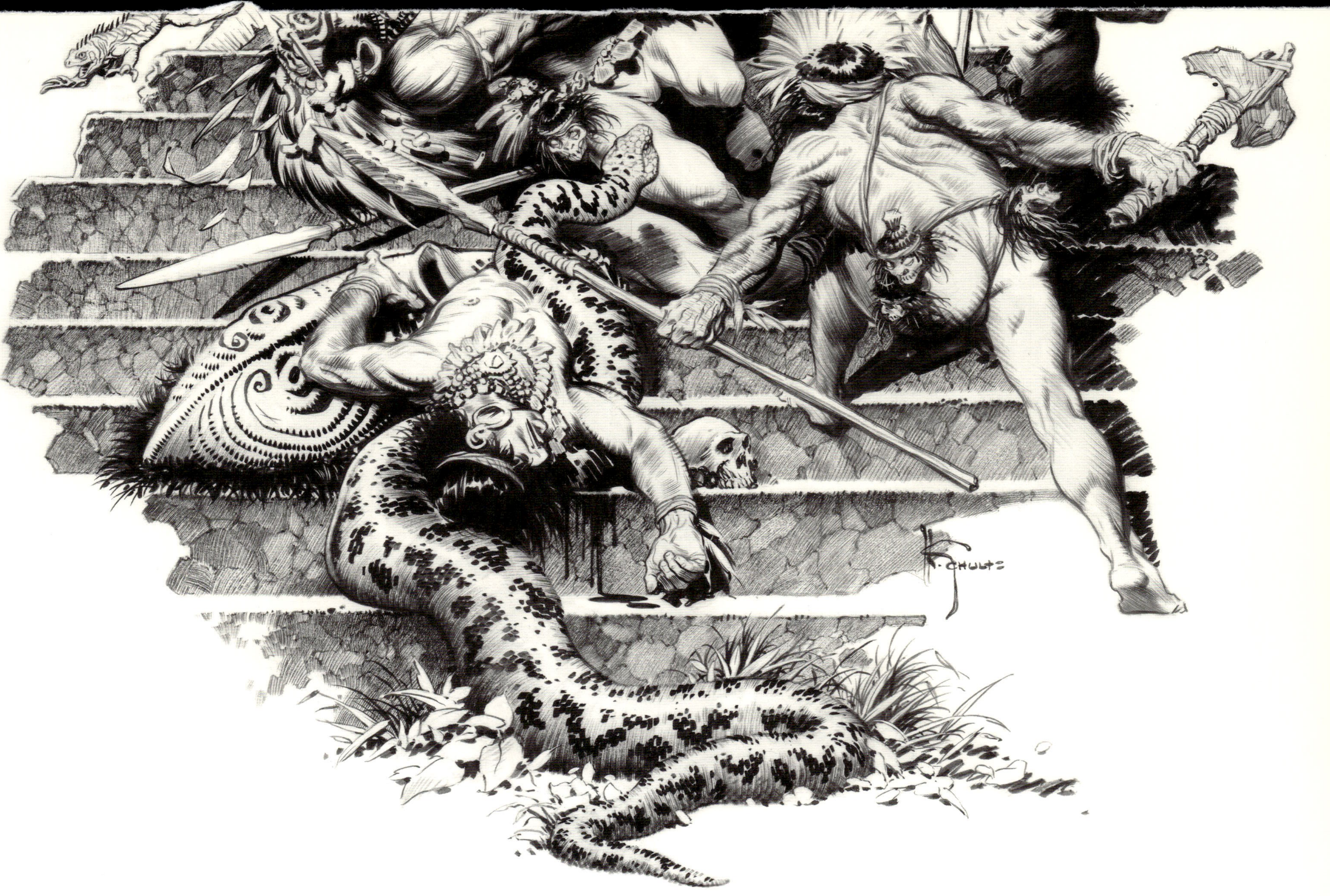

Blanchard Family Picnic completed commission

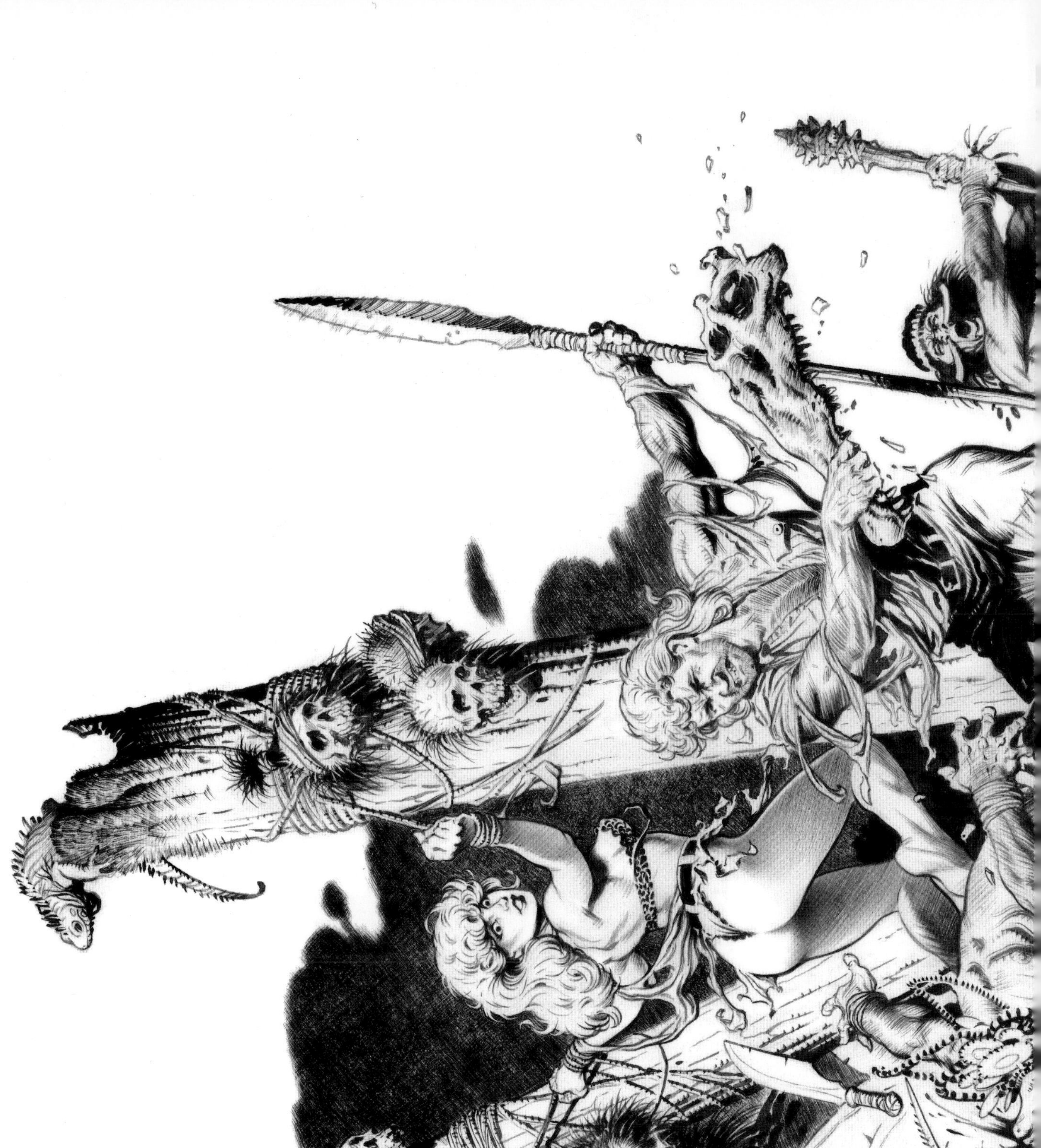

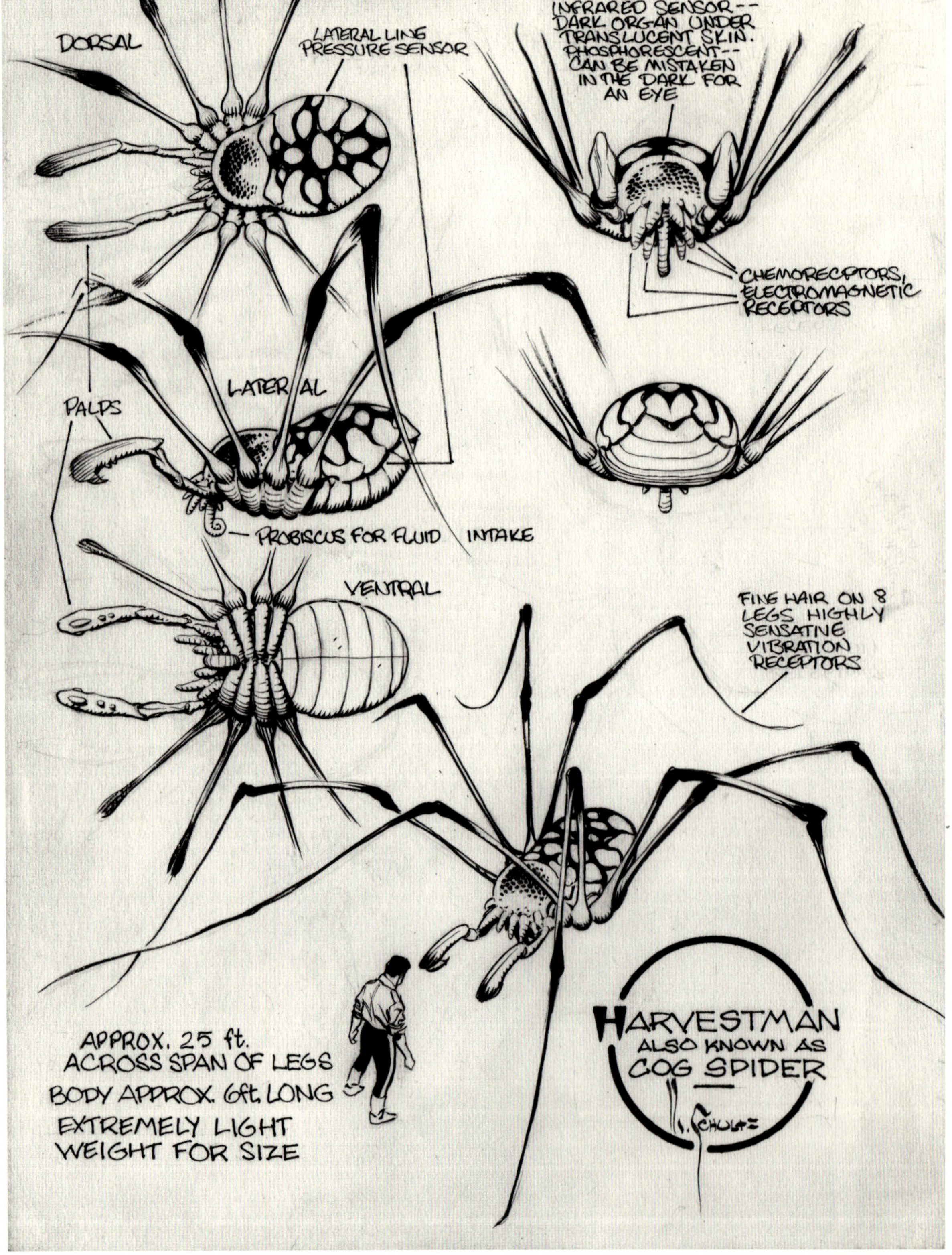

Design sheet: Harvestman, a subterranean creature appearing in *Xenozoic Tales* #14

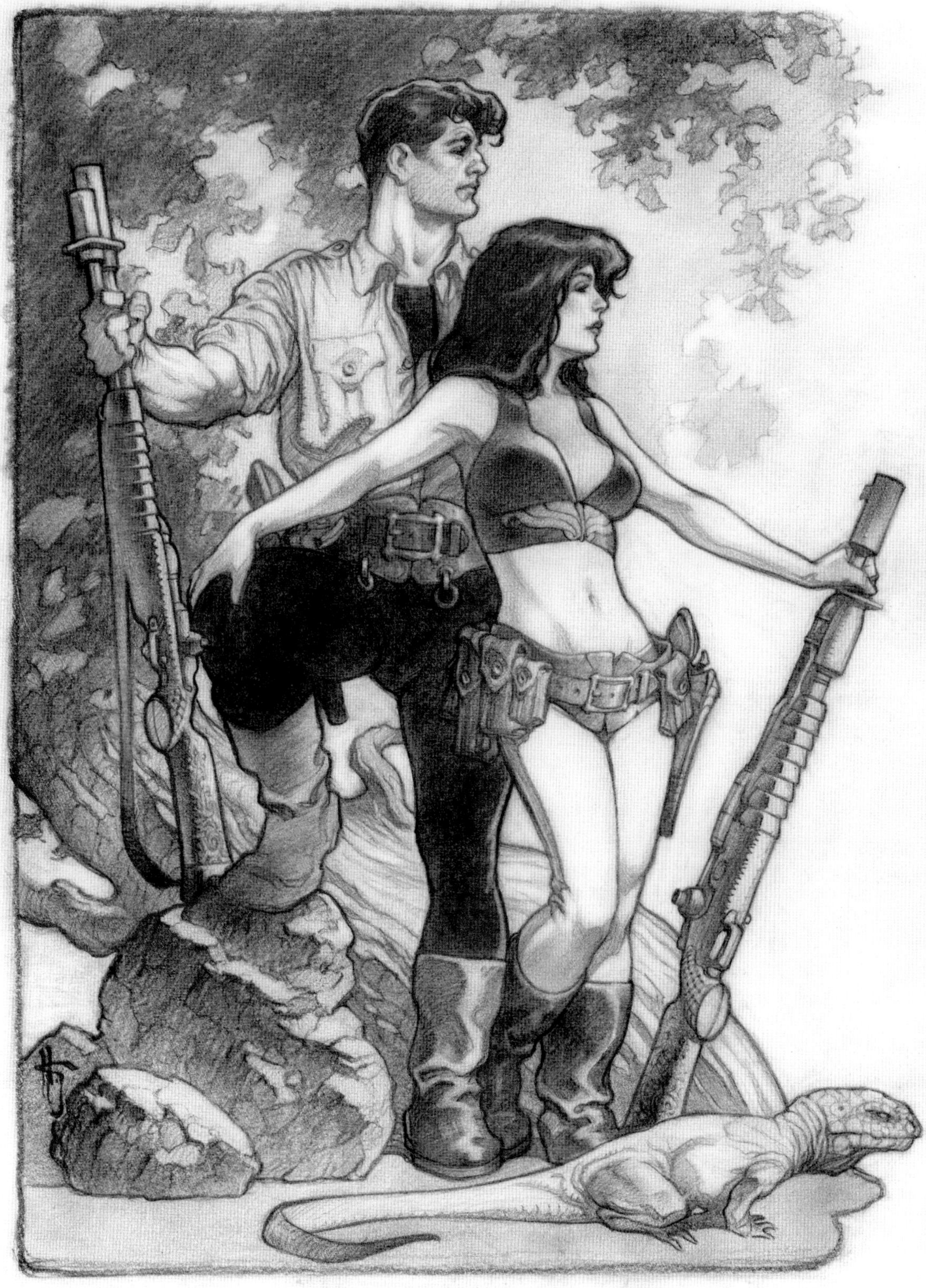

Ms. Hannah Dundee and Mr. Jack Tenrec of *Xenozoic Tales*

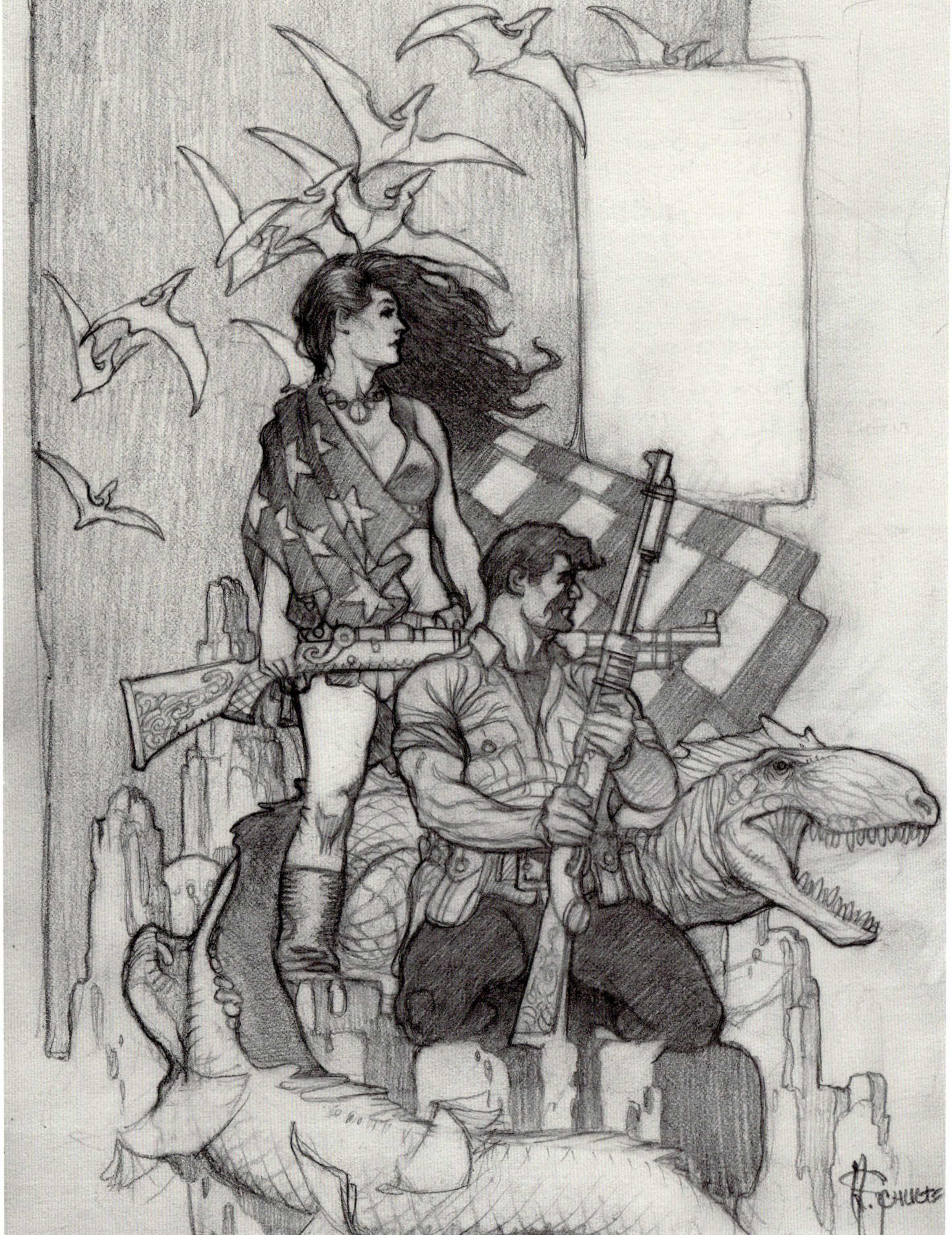

Study for illustration promoting the Comic Book Legal Defense Fund: *More Fund Comics* #1

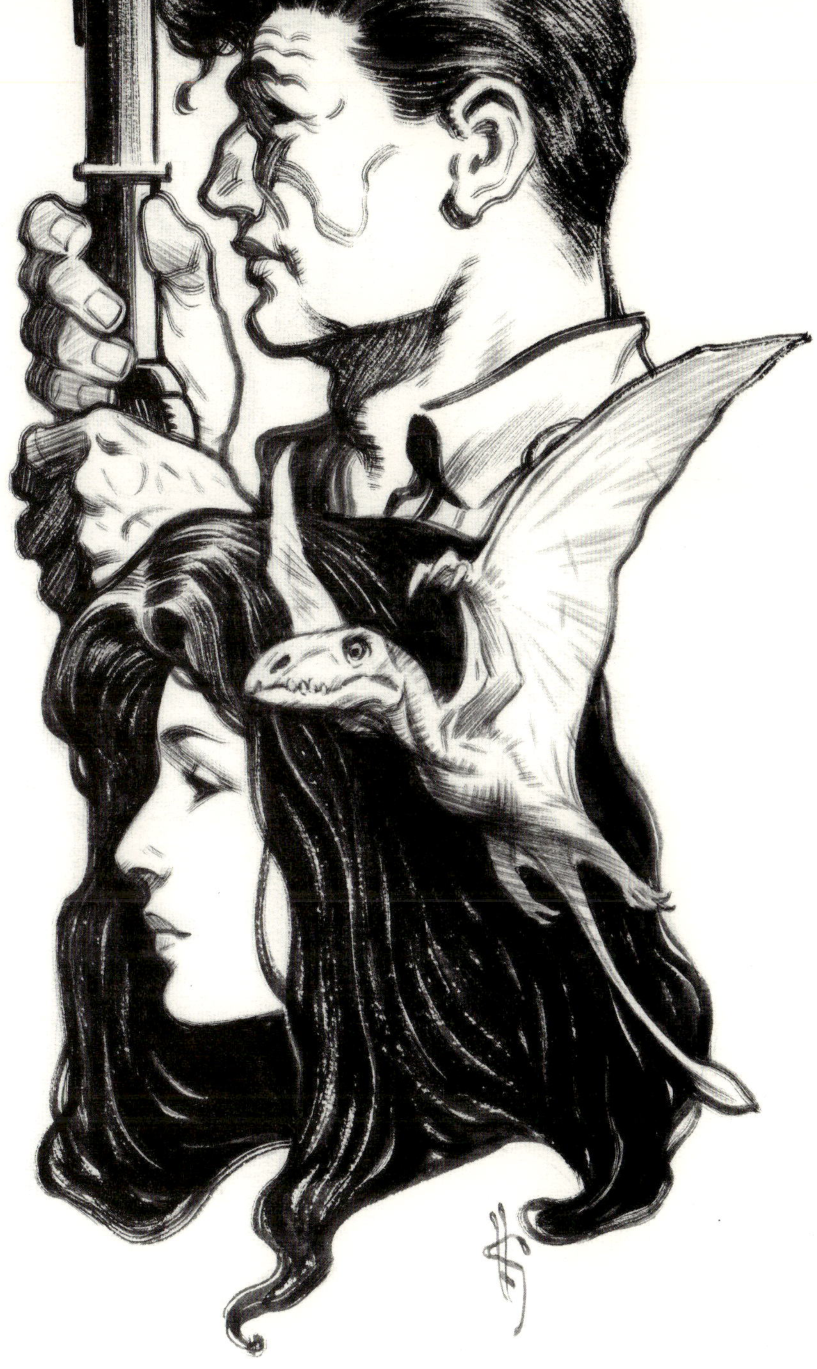

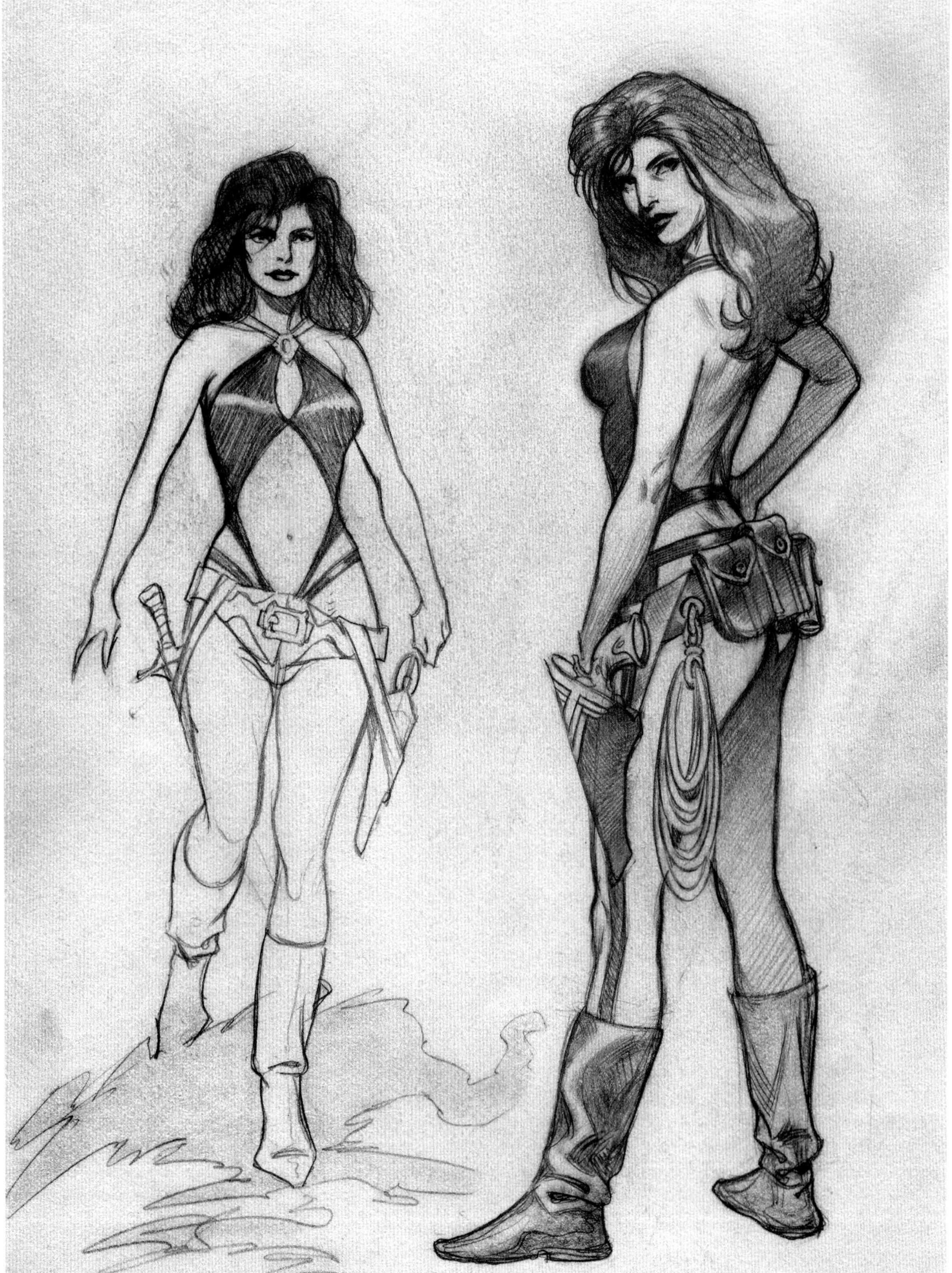

Hannah Dundee costume design, preparation for *Xenozoic Tales* #14

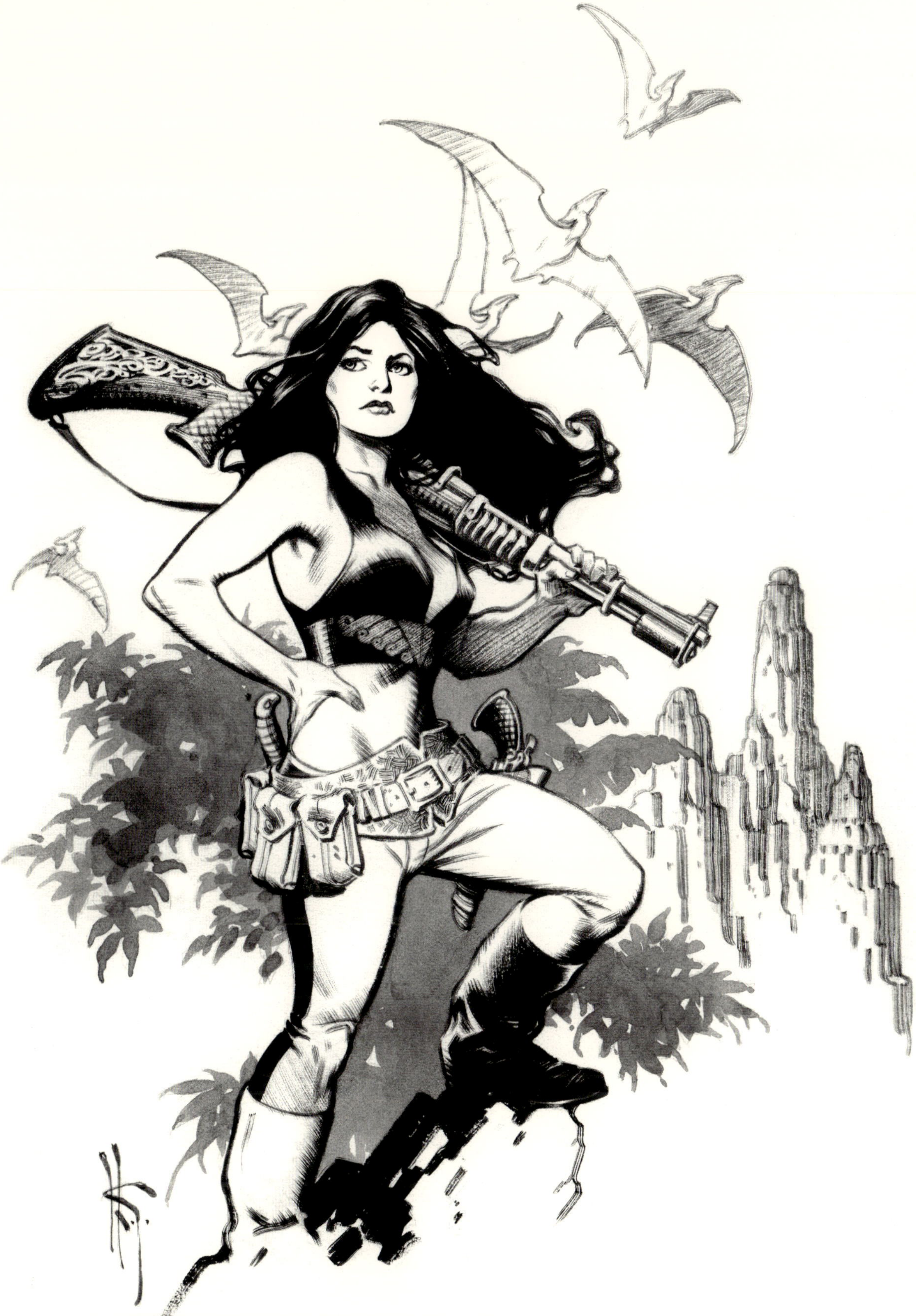

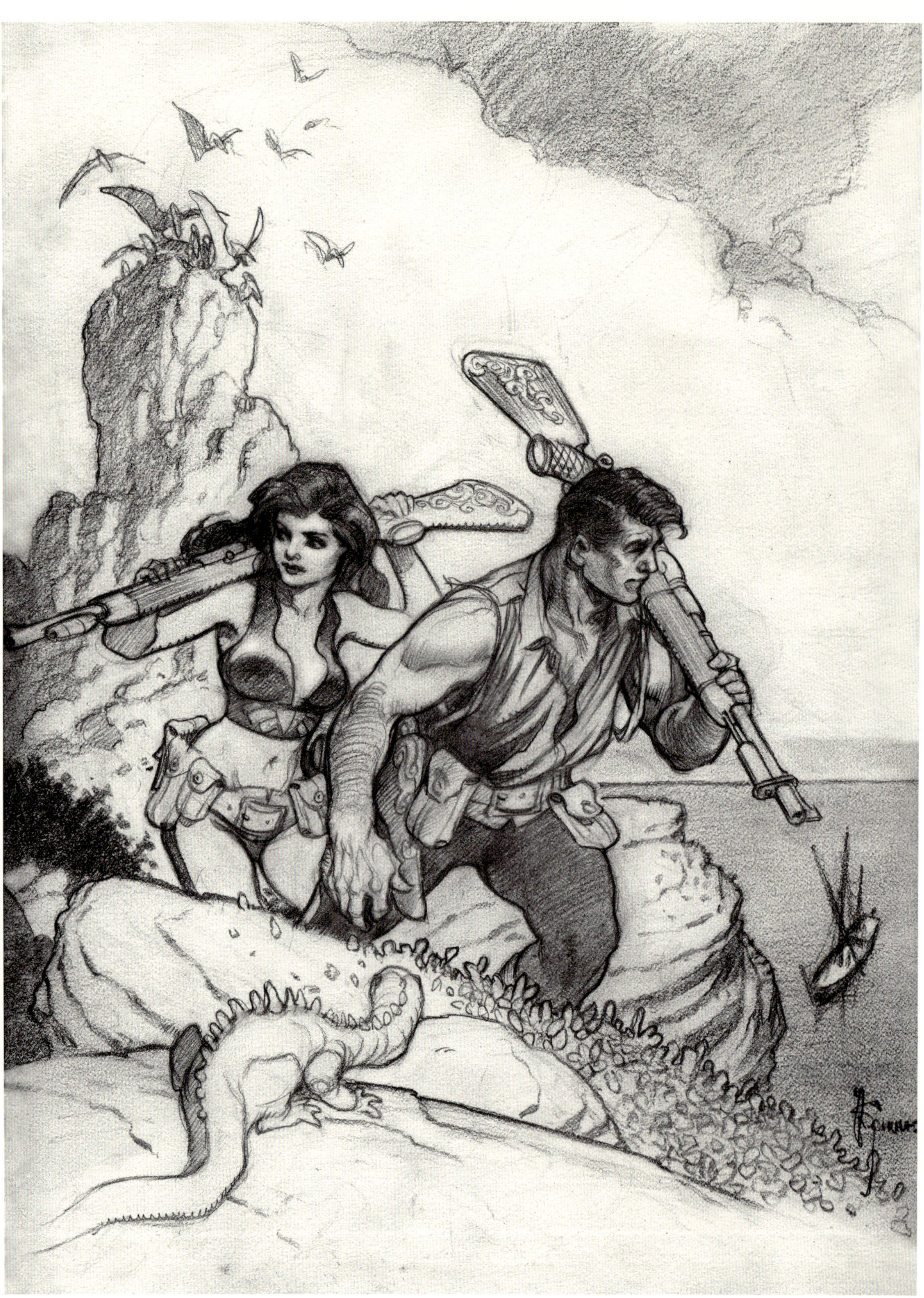

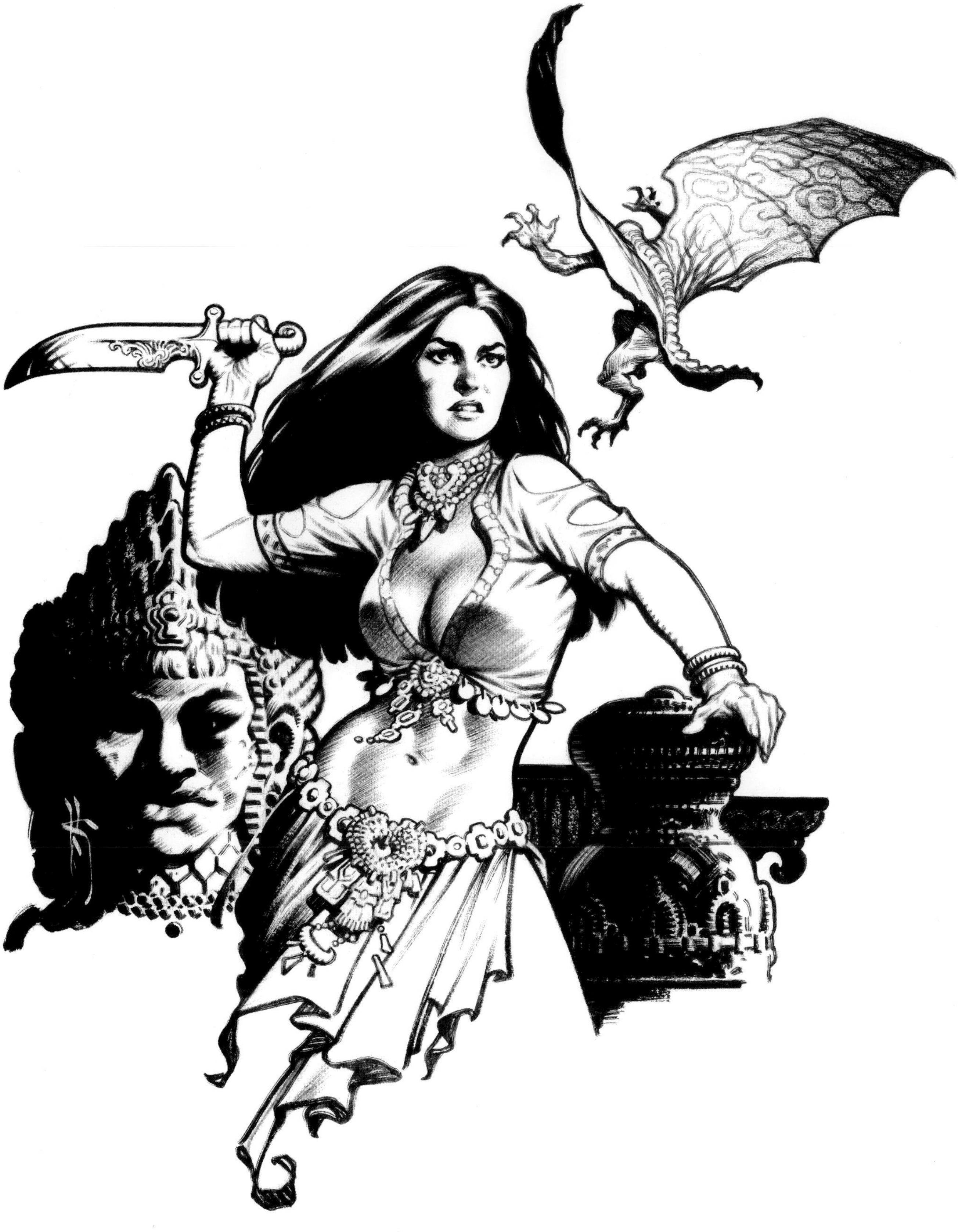

Middle Eastern fantasy: WonderFest convention T-shirt design

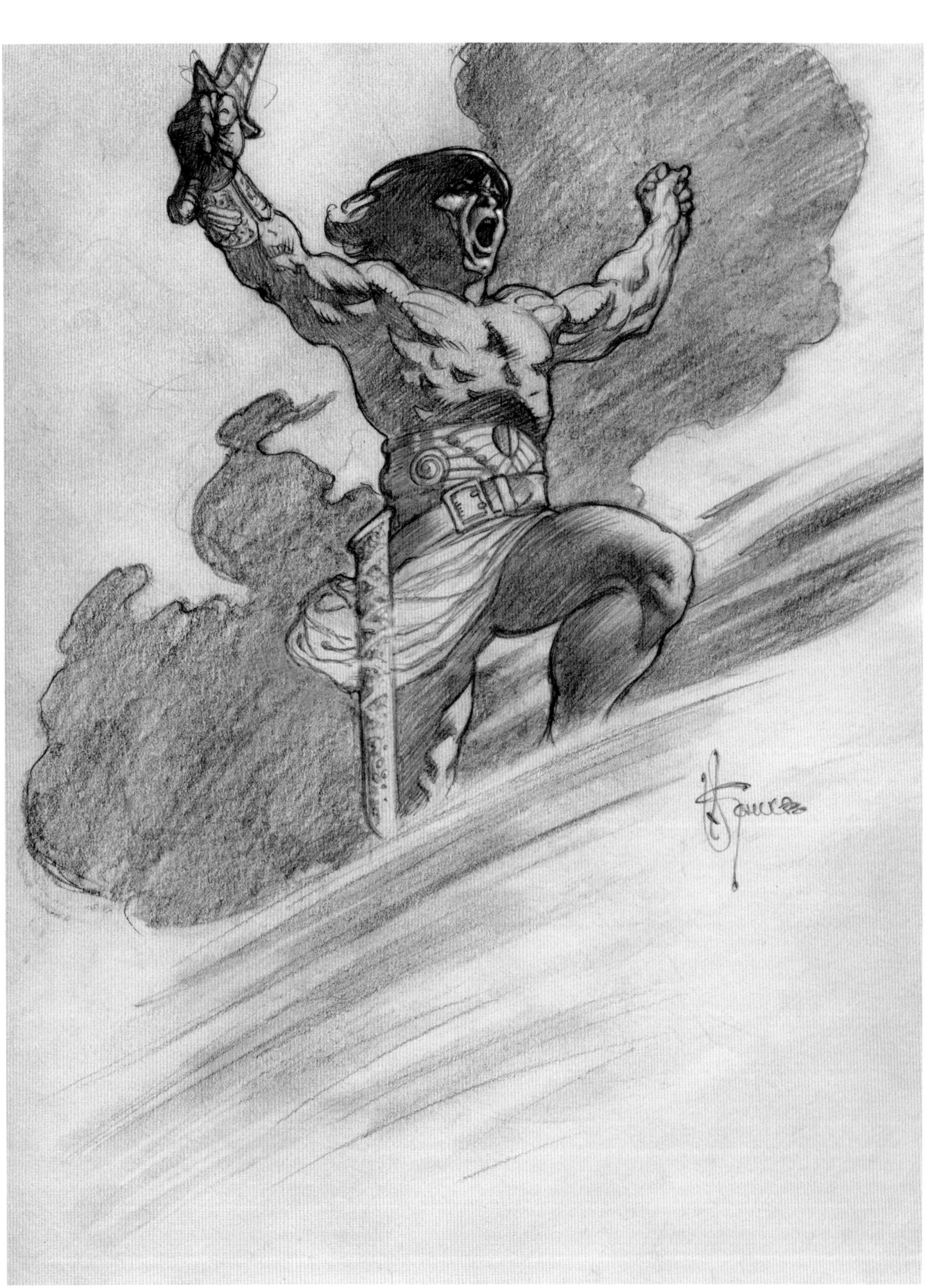

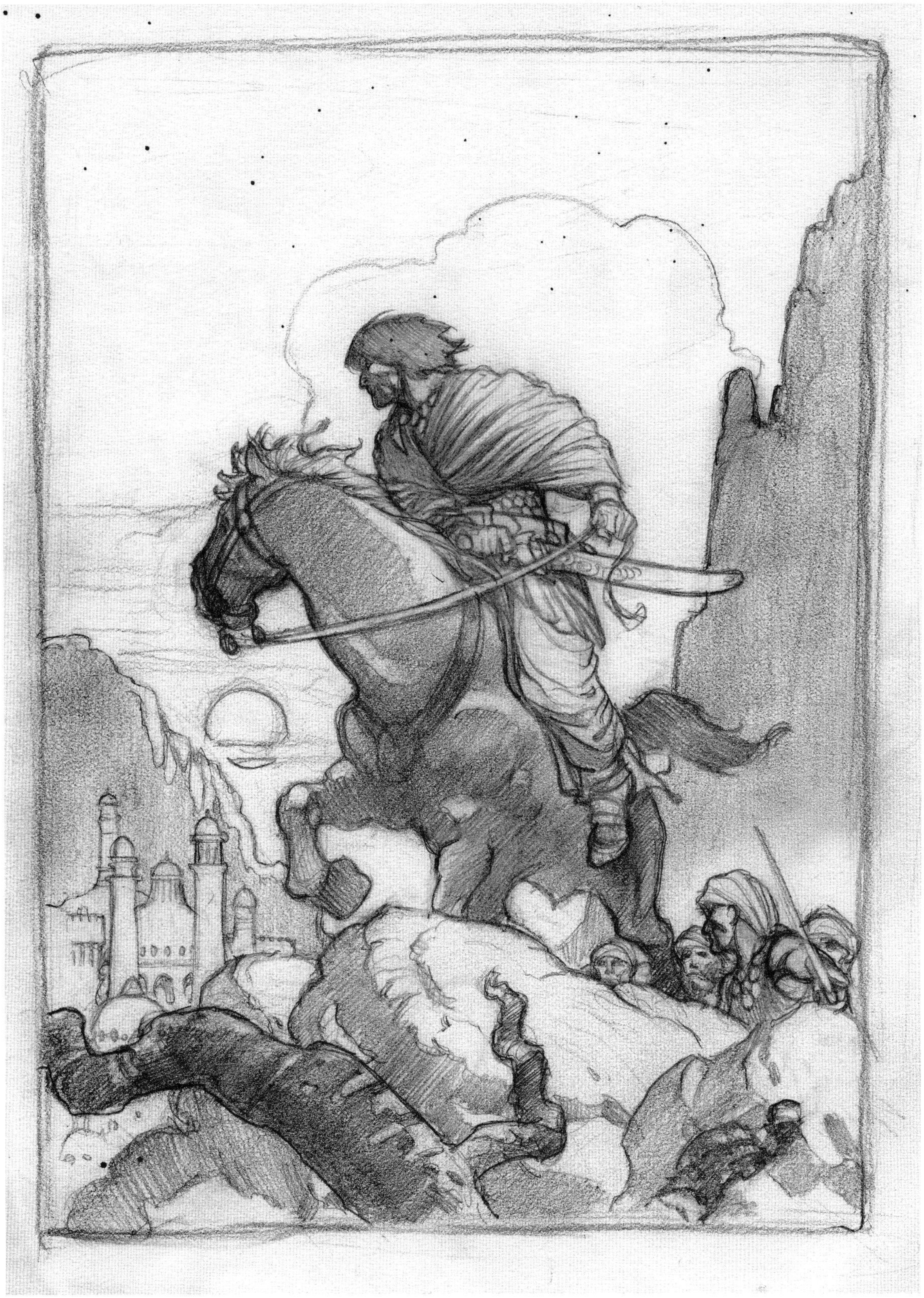

Slipcase painting preliminary:
Robert E. Howard's Complete Conan of Cimmeria, Volume 1

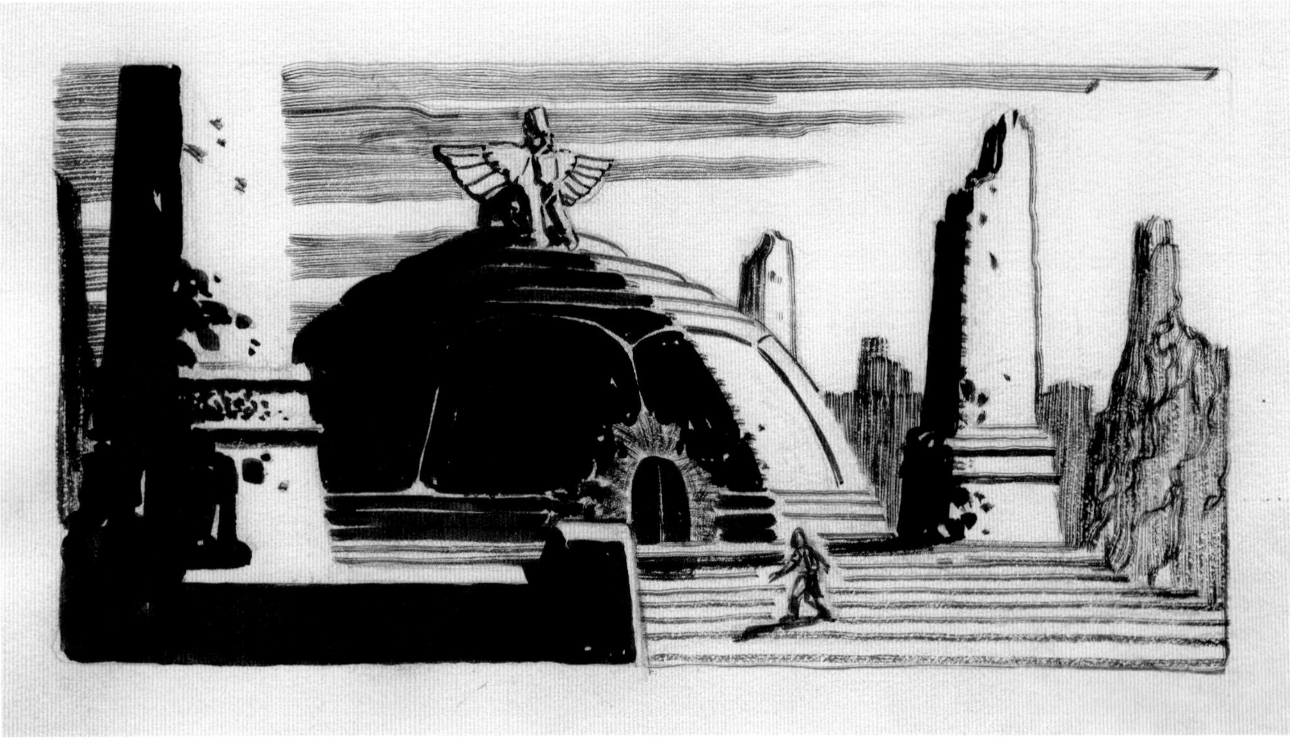

Chapter header preliminaries: Robert E. Howard's *Black Colossus*

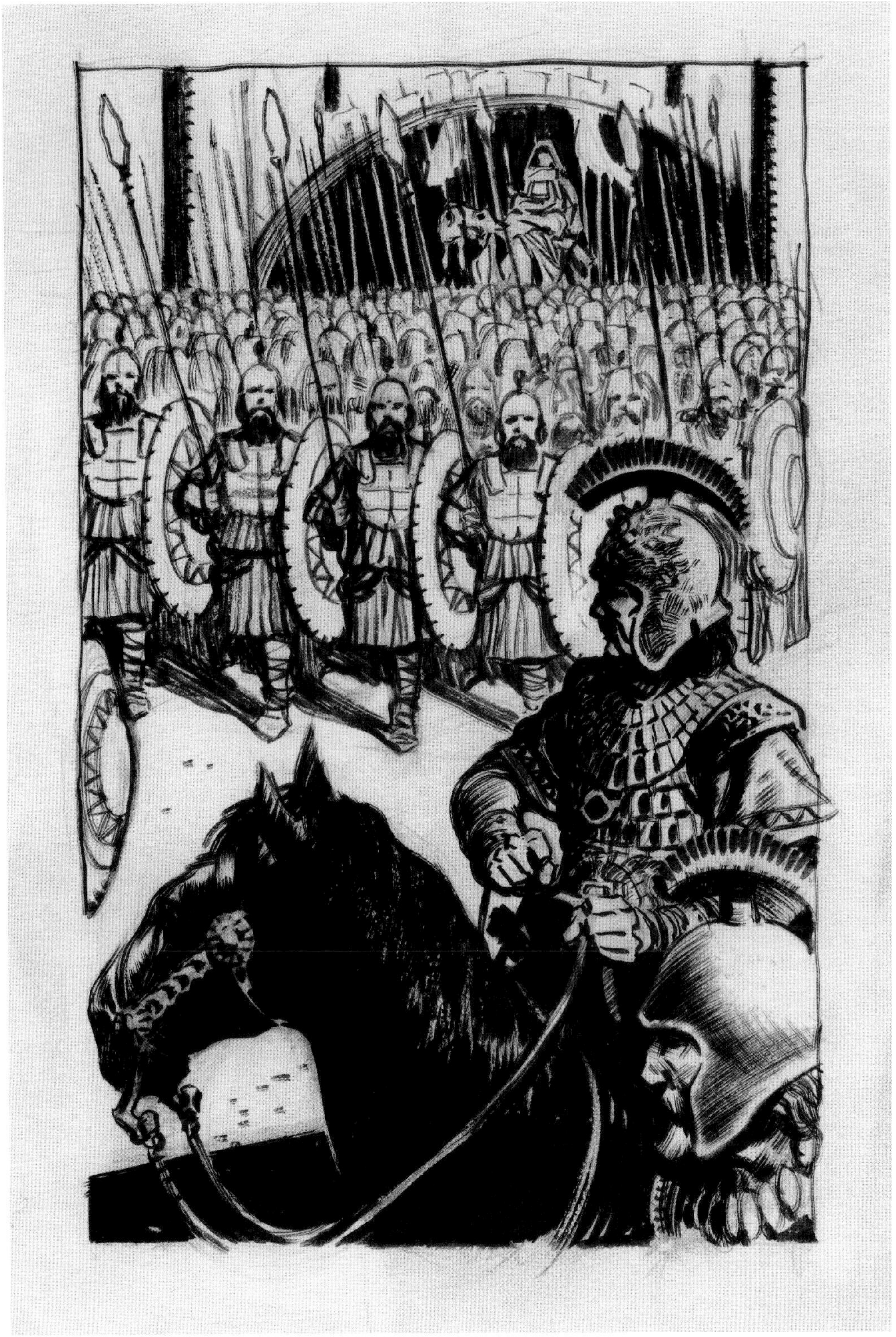

Illustration study: Robert E. Howard's *Black Colossus*

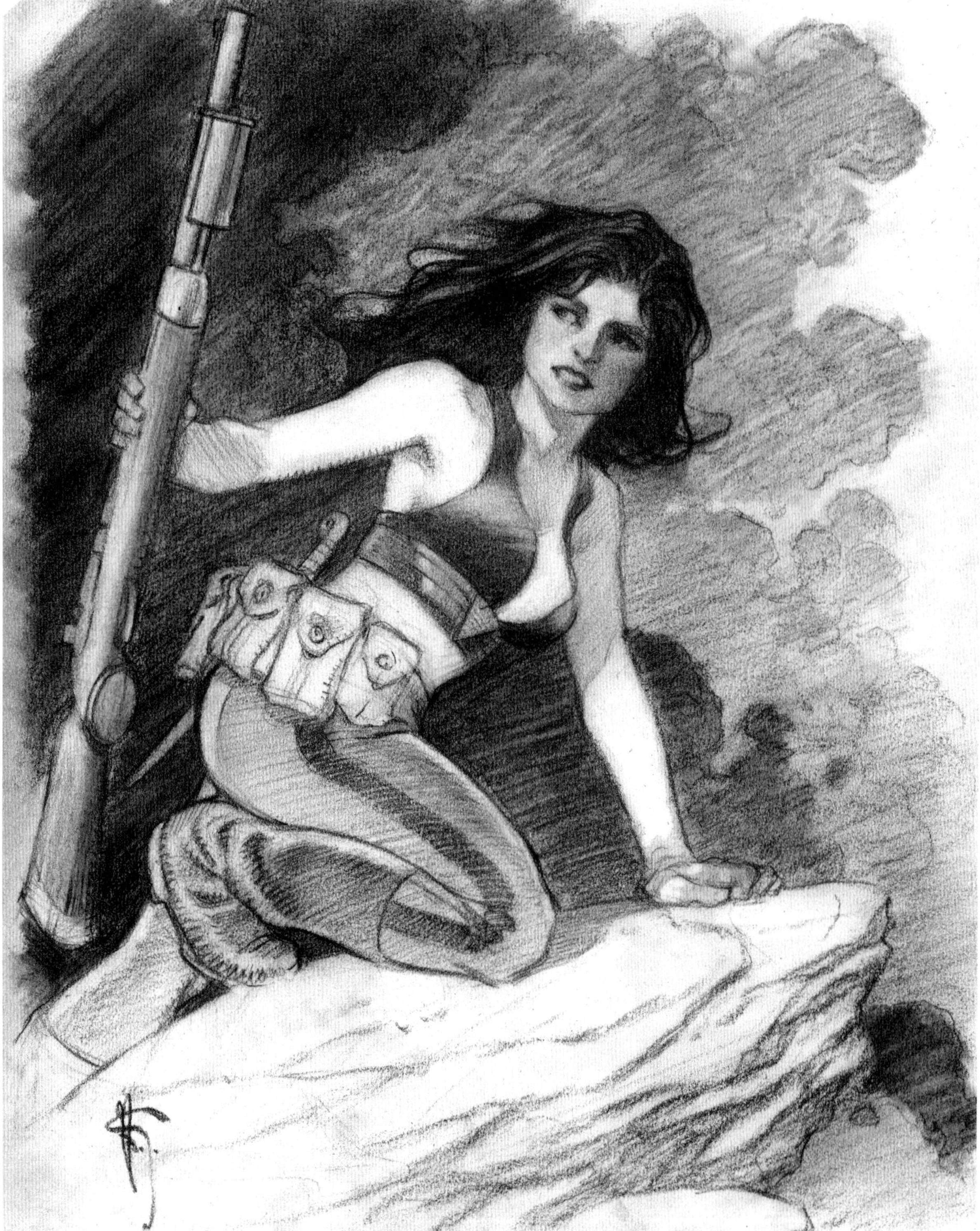

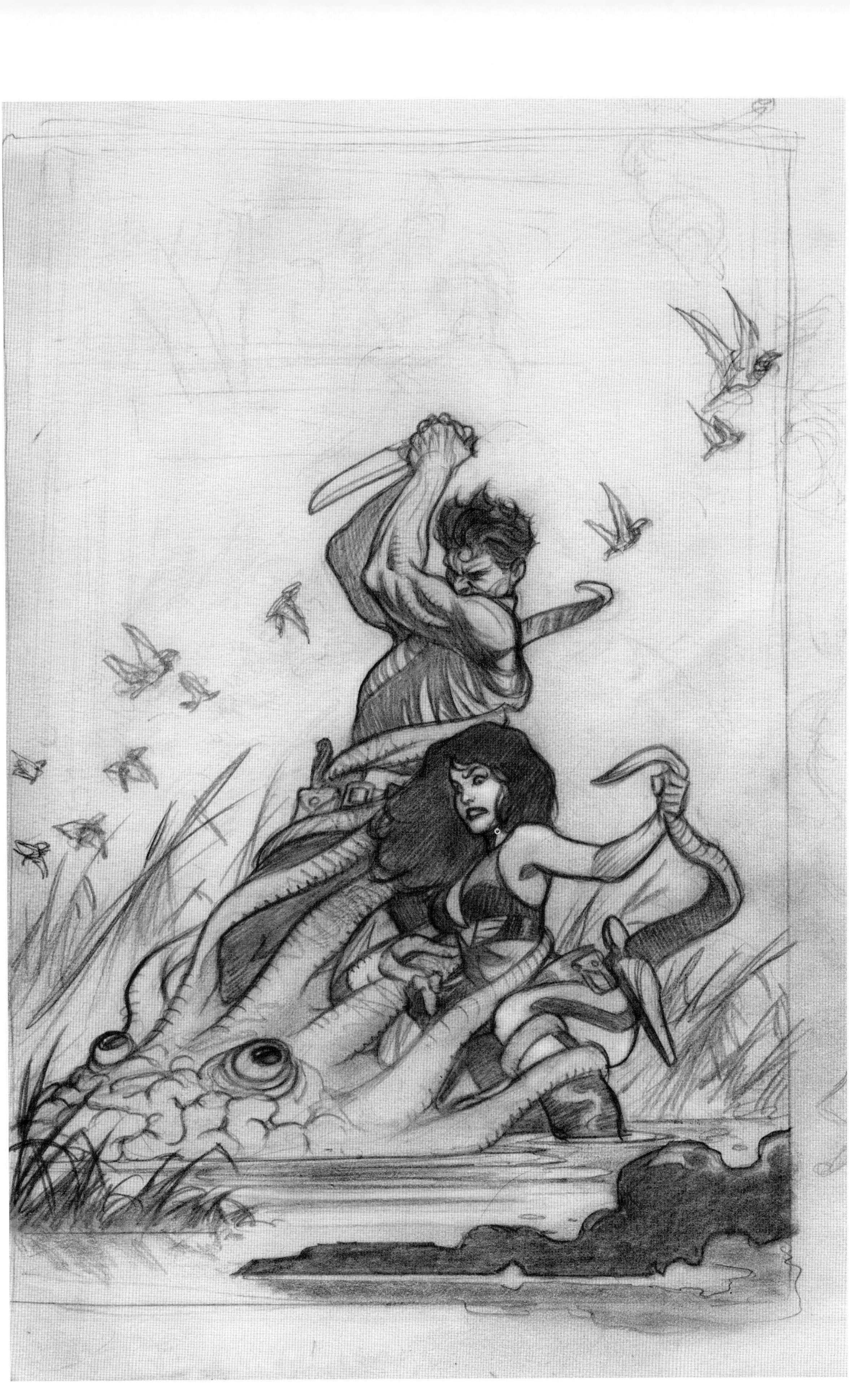

Study for potential cover: *Xenozoic Tales* #15

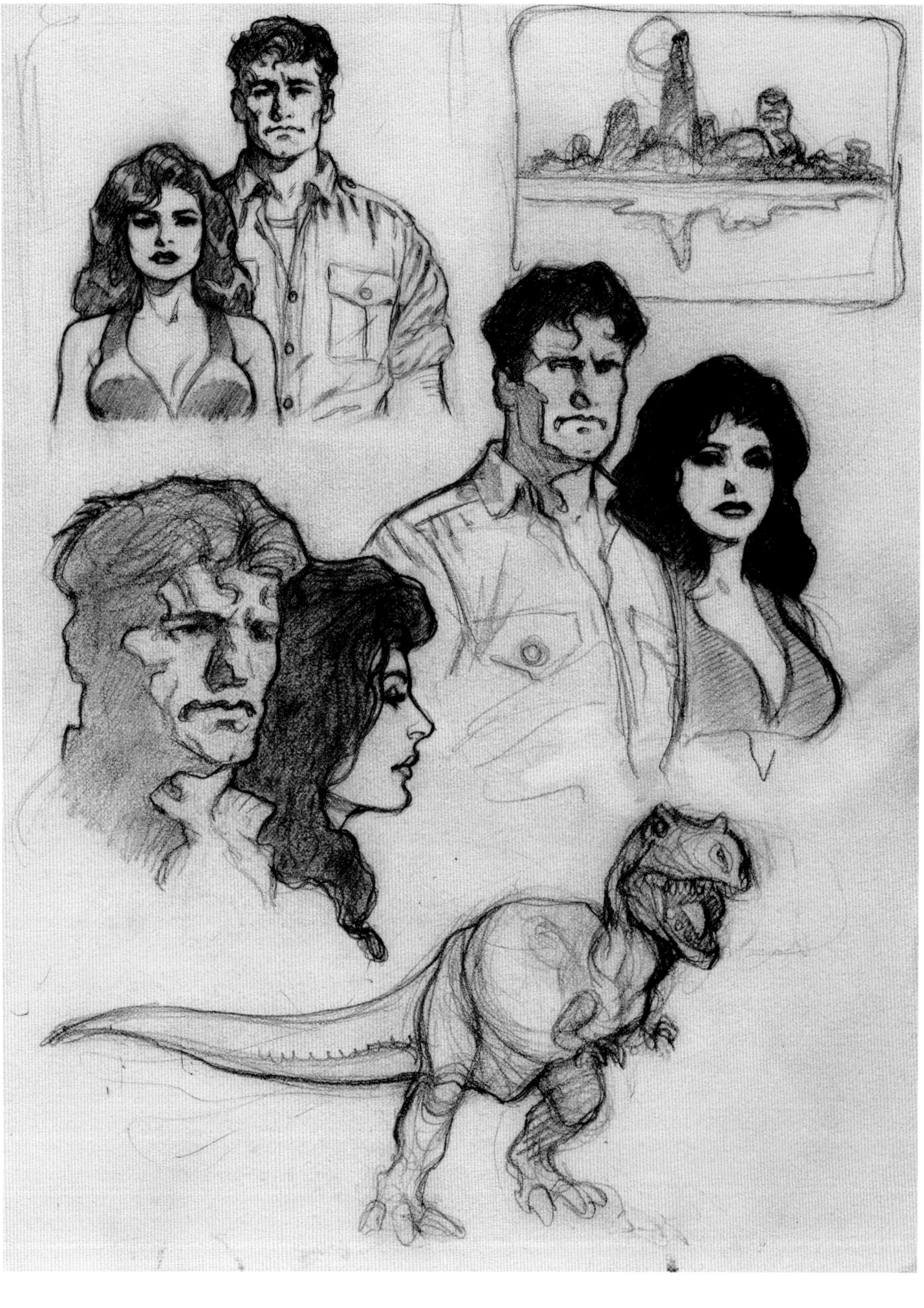

Sketchbook warm-up page

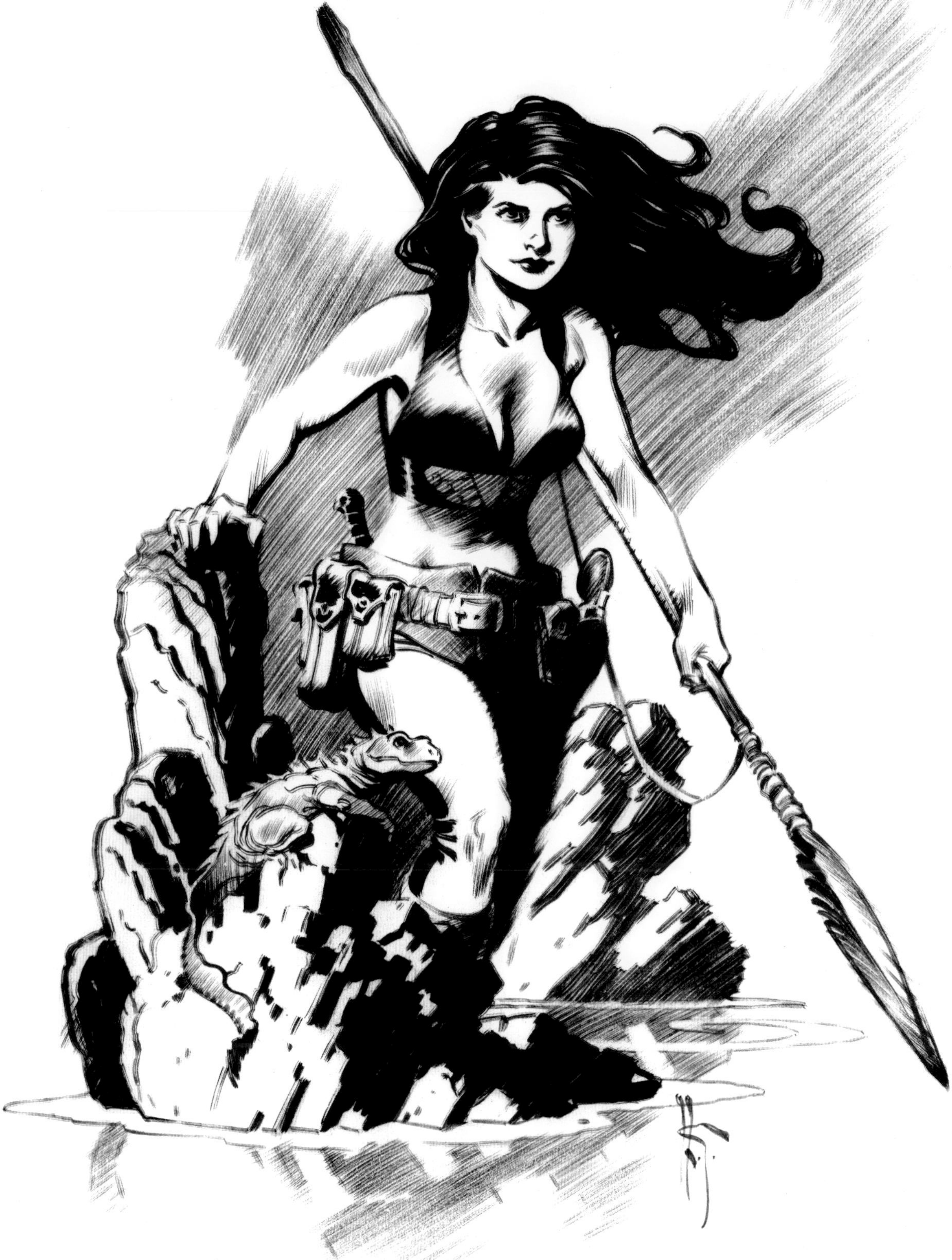

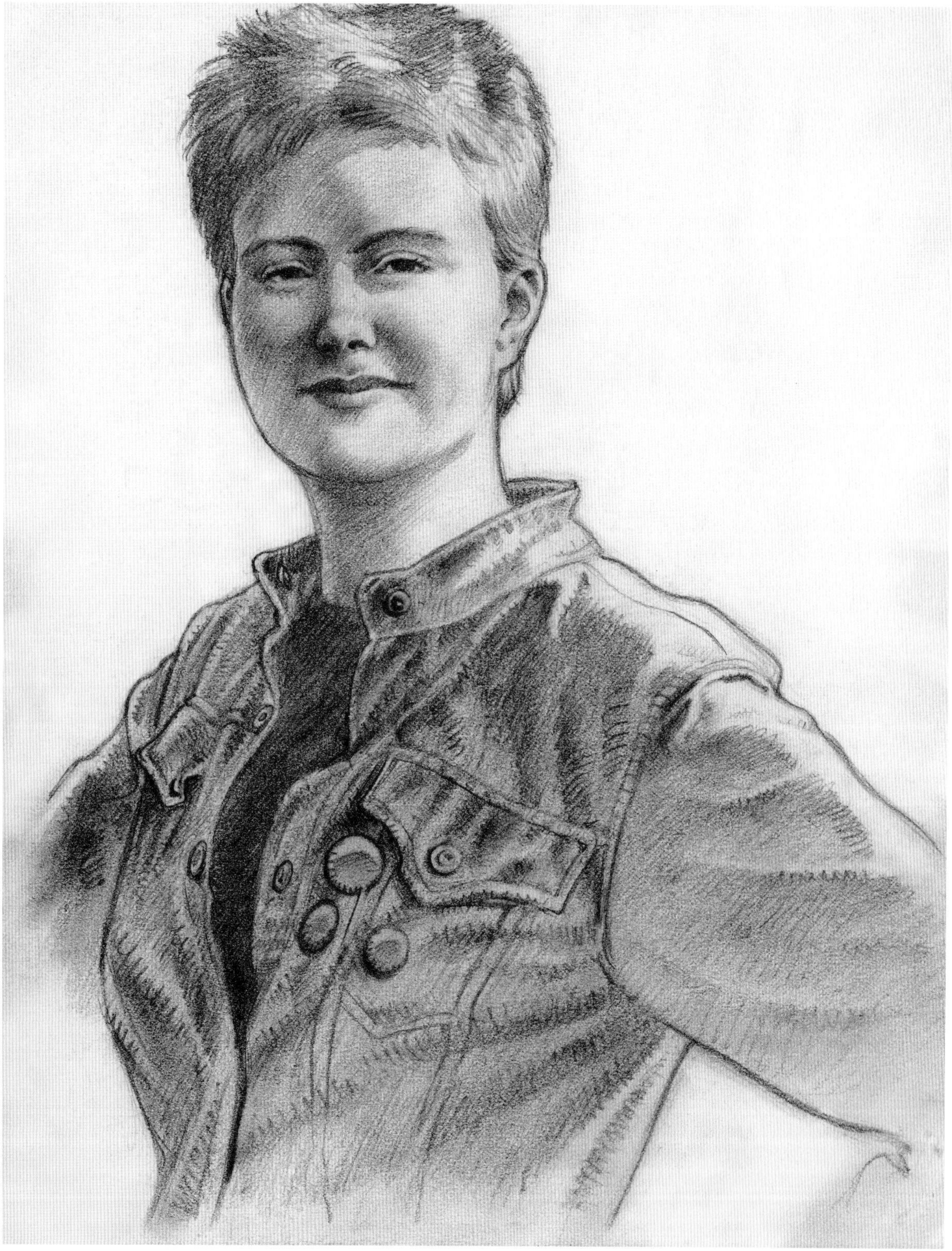

Preliminary study for painted portrait: Shannon

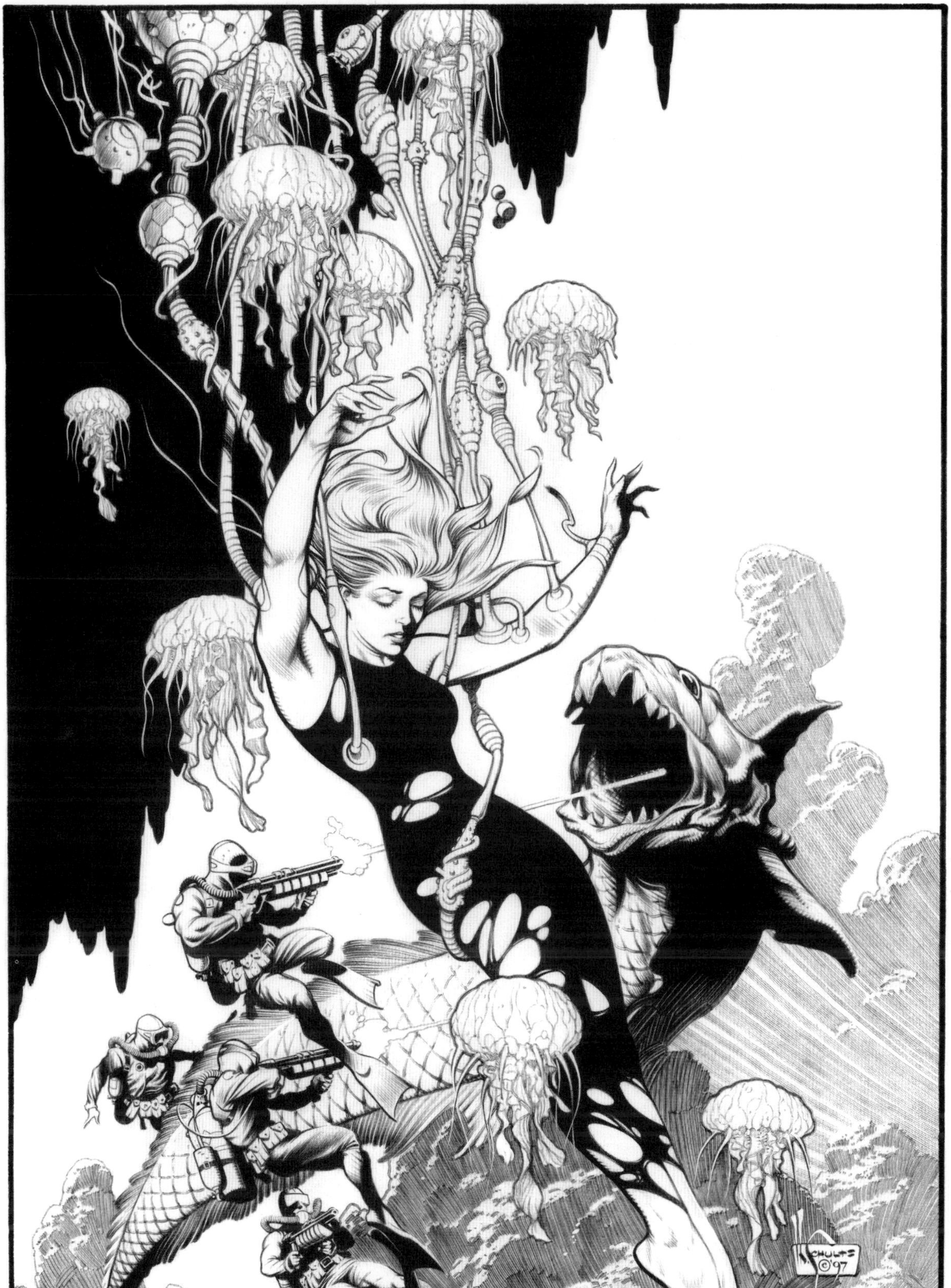

Rejected cover: *SubHuman* #1. Too much of an illustration, not enough of a clearly readable cover design

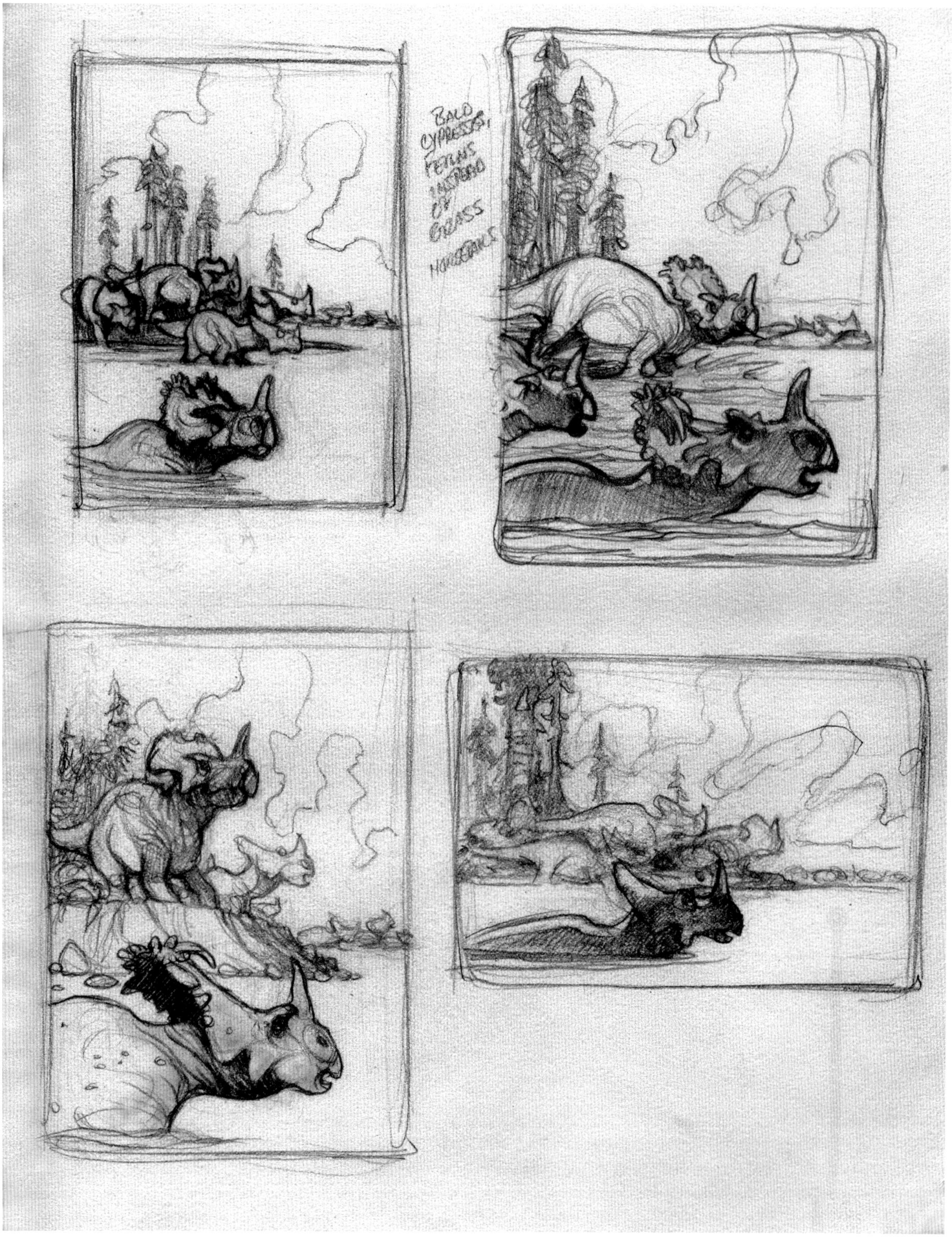

Thumbnailed compositional possibilities:
Centrosaurus from Southern Alberta

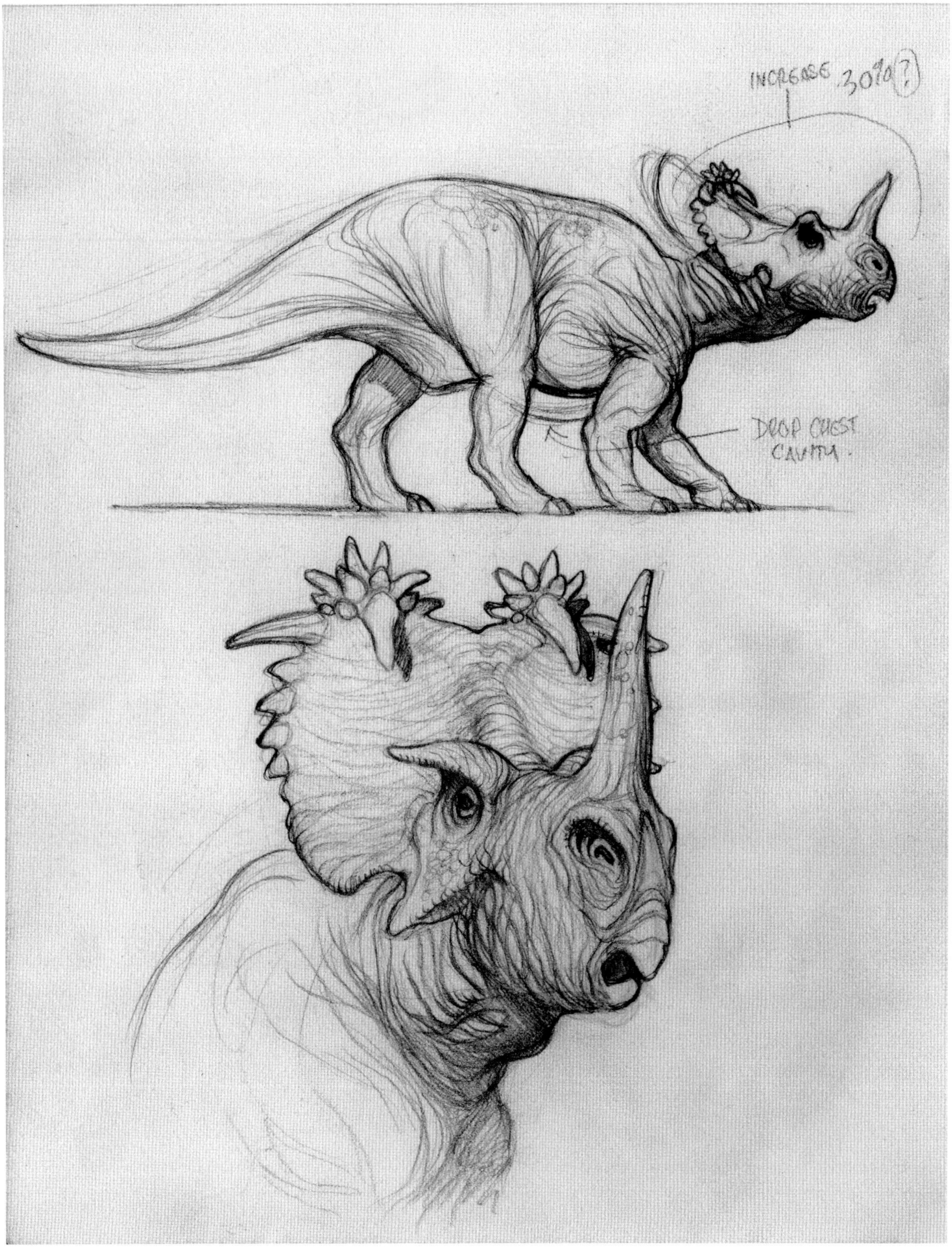

Centrosaurus model studies, prepared under the direction of Michael Ryan, the discoverer of this new species

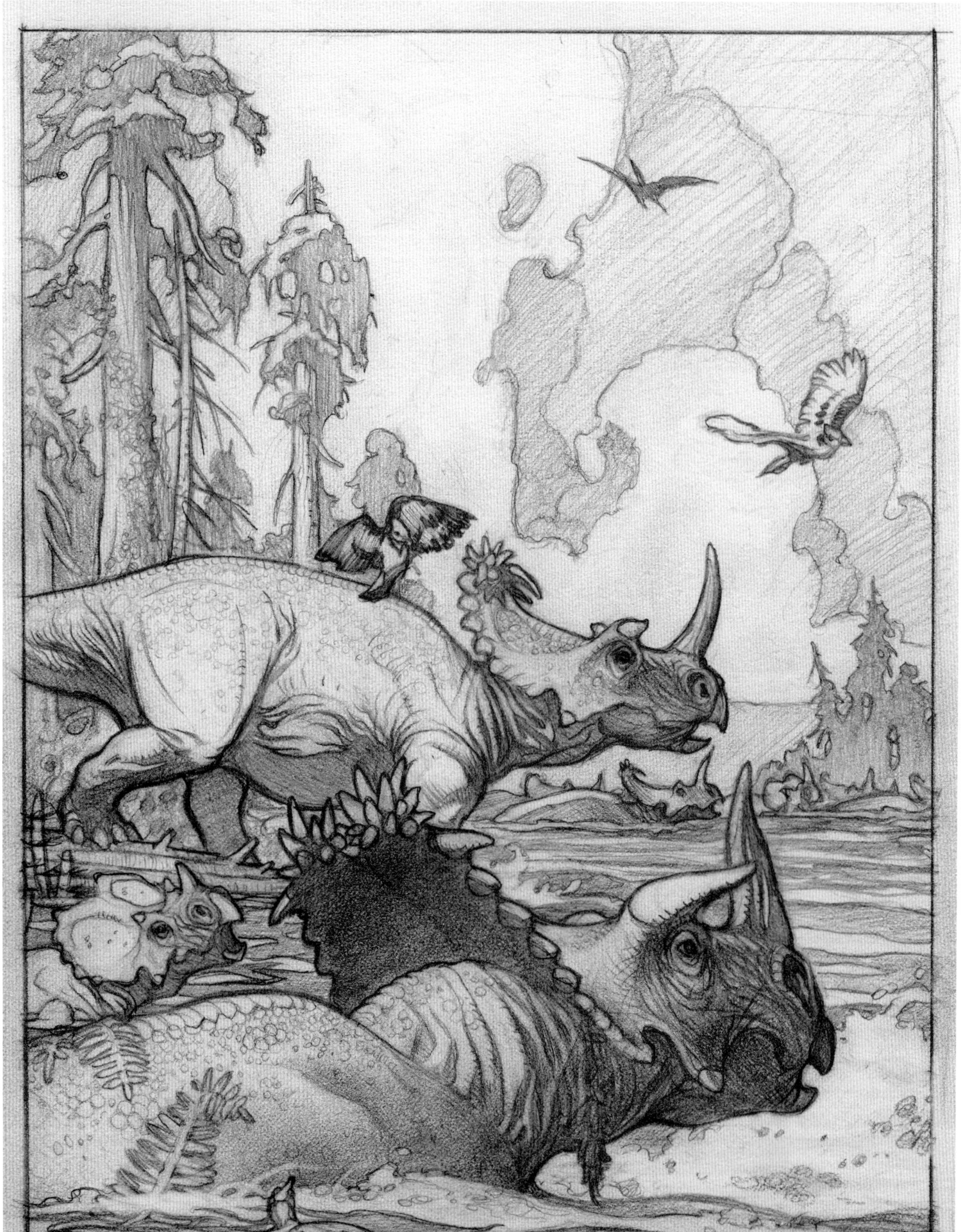

Finalized composition study: *Centrosaurus from Southern Alberta*

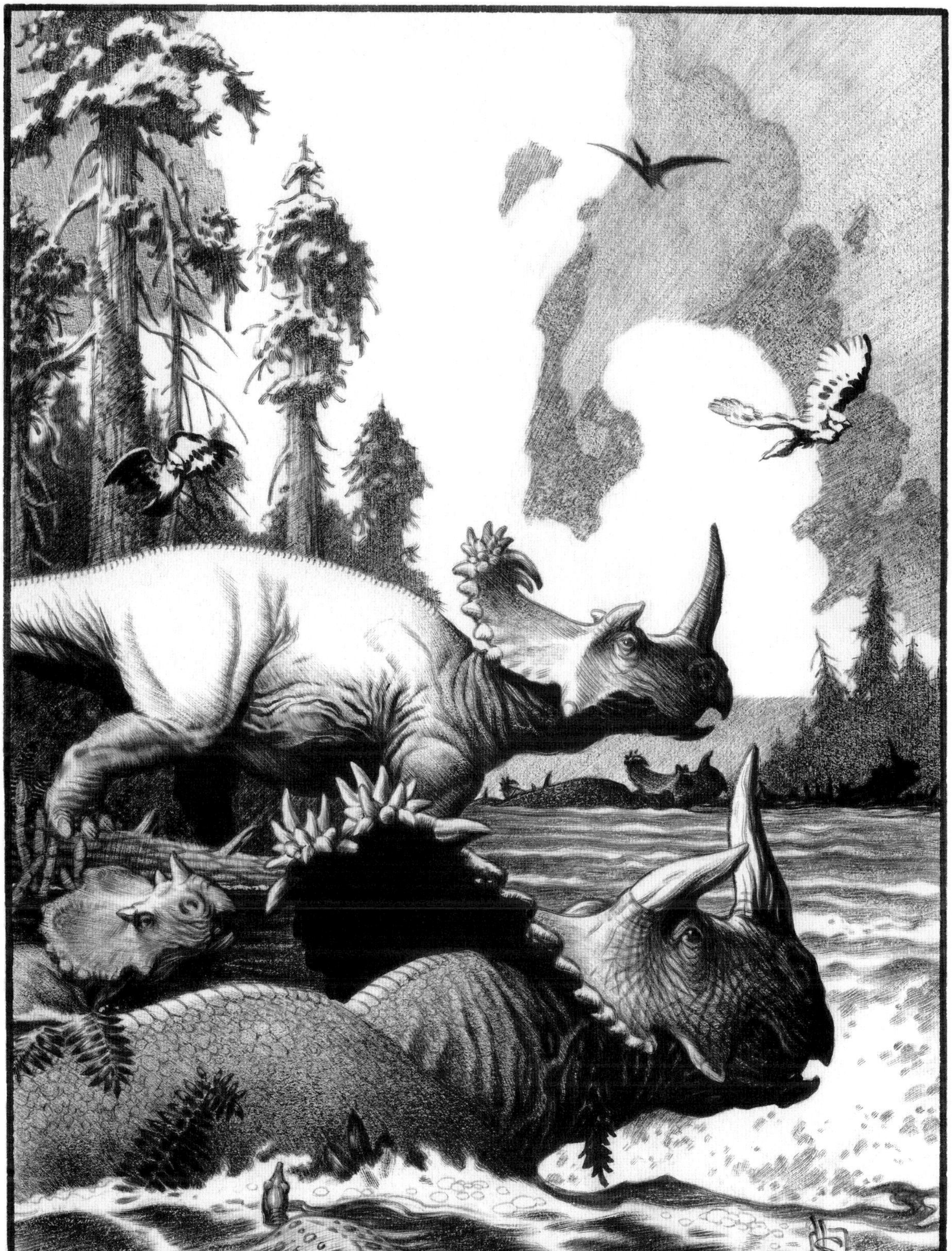

Centrosaurus from Southern Alberta completed commission

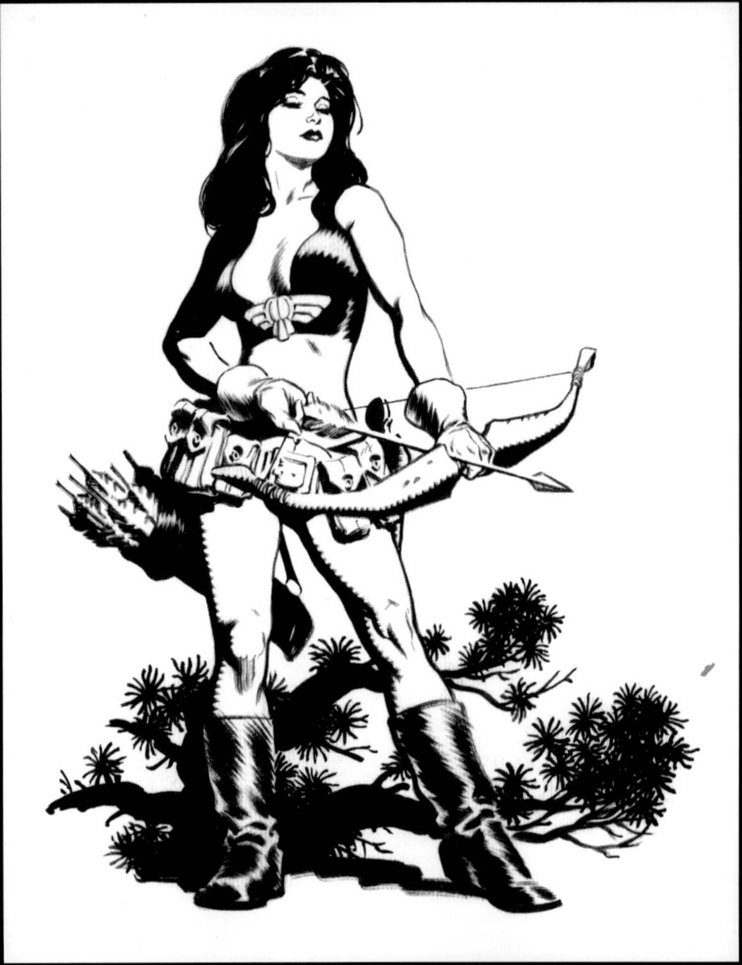